tredition®

www.tredition.de

AF204275

For my daughters

Christoph Werner

TO LIVE IN ALL ETERNITY

CASPAR DAVID FRIEDRICH AND JOSEPH MALLORD WILLIAM TURNER

A Novel

Editor Michael Leonard

www.tredition.de

German Edition:
Um ewig einst zu leben. Bertuch Verlag GmbH Weimar 2006

Preliminary Note
For the scene in London at the beginning of the book the author is indebted to the first chapter of Charles Dickens' novel *Bleak House*. Johann Wolfgang von Goethe's comments about the anti-French nationalism of the Germans are taken from Thomas Mann's *Lotte in Weimar: The Beloved Returns*. The translation of Goethe's *Erlkönig* is by Edgar Alfred Bowring.

Editor: Michael Leonard
Layout: Helga Dreher

© Bertuch Verlag Gmbh Weimar 2006
English edition 2019 by kind permission of Bertuch Verlag GmbH Weimar

Published and printed by tredition GmbH, Hamburg, Halenreie 40-44, 22359 Hamburg

ISBN
978-3-7497-1975-4 (Paperback)
978-3-7497-1976-1 (E-Book)

Table of Contents

PART 1
LONDON, NOVEMBER 1815

CHAPTER 1

There had been bleak autumn weather for weeks. The smoke from the chimneys, instead of rising up and disappearing, sank down on the dirty streets and mixed with fog and soot, becoming a ghastly black drizzle of such depressing weight that it seemed the sun would never shine again.

Dirt and mud covered the streets so that horses drawing coaches and carts were splashed to their very blinders. Cold damp fog lay everywhere, penetrated everything and seemed to drive out all warmth from clothes and coats and shoes and hands.

People hurried to escape the drizzle and mud, often colliding with their umbrellas. No one apologized and all seemed ill-tempered. At the corners, many slipped in the wet morass, and reaching out for support only managed to pull another pedestrian down.

The sedan-bearers above all had great trouble conveying their human freight undamaged to their destinations, and mumbled swear words to themselves, if the gentleman or the lady who they carried were of too weighty a corpulence.

Those bearers who did not wear numbers showing official registration were probably the servants of the ladies and gentlemen in the chairs, therefore less skilled and more likely to put their masters and mistresses in jeopardy through a sudden slip. Still, the sedan-chairs were preferred to the coaches, because they fitted better through narrow alleyways and allowed them to be carried into their very houses. Thus, neither the shoes nor the coiffures of the ladies or the silken coats of the gentlemen were compromised.

Among the hired servants, scribes, housewives, maids, coal hikers, students, parliamentary clerks, artisans, Thames fishermen, merchant apprentices and pickpockets, the most conspicuous characters were the chimney sweeps, mostly boys, completely black, who lugged along their brushes and bags full of soot, which their masters sold as fertilizer.

The sweeps were small and slim in order to fit through the chimneys. They climbed in from the bottom, and their jobs were done only when their heads emerged at the top. If they did not work fast enough or did not dare climb far enough into the narrow and winding chimneys, their masters encouraged them by lighting a small fire below, which accelerated their efforts in a most desired way.

If the children grew too large, they were no longer employable as sweeps. Yet this rarely occurred because burns, injuries and malignant growths on the boys' testicles, called soot warts, put an early end to their lives, which their masters judged to be a willful impertinence because a replacement now had to be located who was as cheap and willing to work as their dead mates.

In fact, new blood was not hard to find; impoverished or alcoholic parents often sold children as young as four years old for twenty or thirty shillings.

The cold November fog was particularly hard on these skinny little figures, a few girls among them, who had only the old clothes and rags begged from families of the better-off. And if they were not able to avoid the litter-bearers and the other grown-ups, they were cursed, called beggars, dawdlers and felons, and roughly pushed out of the way.

After delivering their soot and perhaps begging food from the house owners, they had to find a dark corner, often the entrance to a basement or an old vault, crept into their soot bags in order to sleep and gather strength for the next day.

The clever ones found sleeping-places away from the bright light of the gas lamps recently erected in some streets, particularly in the city of Westminster, but they had to be wary of the night watchmen patrolling the streets between 9 o'clock at night and sunrise, who checked on all suspicious persons.

The painter Joseph Mallord William Turner, Royal Academician and professor of perspective at the Royal Academy, walked unnoticed through the crowd. He wore a top-hat, and against the vile cold a white woolen muffler, a long dark coat and solid brown boots. He seemed aloof from what went on around him, but in fact was extremely attentive. Seeing the small sweeps with their bags he remembered William Blake's verses:

And so Tom awoke;
and we rose in the dark,
and got with our bags
and our brushes to work.
Though the morning was cold,
Tom was happy and warm;

so if all do their duty
they need not fear harm.

Strange fellow, this Blake, Turner thought. Poet and painter, crazy, but still an ingenious and independent spirit and a talented engraver. His occupation with the art of engraving led to his overestimation of the line, the drawing, the distinction between figure and object, which was for him almost a question of morality. As a consequence, Blake put less value on color and light and shade.

But truly, is not the indefinite, the impression, the real mirror of life?

Still, he believed Blake's picture *Pity* from '95, a watercolor done in pen and ink, in which all his principles find their expression, showed a peculiar kind of progressiveness, which would be taken up and continued by the painters of future generations, as they would one day understand his, Turner's, differing ideas on the art of painting.

Turner had just come from Coleman Street in the Docklands, where he regularly frequented a brothel. At the same time, he had used the opportunity to collect rent for the flats and houses in Wapping, which he had inherited from the family of his mother. Of course, he could not get rich this way, as for example the big magnate John Russell, who was able to finance his agricultural innovations by the proceeds he received from his possession of Bloomsbury in the middle of London.

Turner loved combining the useful with the pleasant. In the brothel he enjoyed the physical pleasures offered to him as well as the interesting positions the female forms were able to assume during their service.

He rarely left this establishment without having sketched the women, both during their services to him and afterward.

Because he believed that hardly anyone would understand what relief from the bourgeois and hypocritical respectability of the day these visits brought him, if only for a short time, this sketchbook was kept safely under lock and key, and additionally provided with metal clasps in order to make it difficult for unauthorized persons to view the drawings. To achieve this, he did not shy away from spending freely, though normally he had acquired the habit of being economical with his money.

Coming from the brothel that day, he was still amused by the answer a Thames angler had given him in a most engaging Cockney slang after being asked if he had caught any fish. 'Lawd above! No, gov'nor, I 'aven't. There's no need. 'elps me ter get away from da wife fer a few 'aaahrs, innit.'

In this respect the painter had fared better. He had been cautious and not taken a wife at all. Secretly, he had had a relationship with Sarah, the widow of John Danby, the well-known organist and composer, for more than fifteen years, but still could not bring himself to marry her, though she had born him two daughters, Evelina and Georgianna.

Women to him were too mysterious; they had such strange wishes and demanded unspoken understanding, though on the other hand were fond of many words. They were capable of

14

emotional outbursts that devastated his nerves and had even afflicted his mother so greatly that he and his father had had to put her, years ago, into a madhouse. And even his daughters he rarely saw after they had grown up. He had felt unable to cope with the strange physical and mental changes that attended their growth and development.

On the other hand, he loved the female body. It was alluring and exotic and provided him with great physical bliss, but women sooner or later wanted to build a nest and make it the center of their and his lives, and therefore he could not allow a wife to disturb or interfere with his work. So, he chose to stay alone where the center of his existence was his studio.

For the three miles from Wapping to Somerset House where the Royal Academy was located, he had allowed himself a coach. He alighted in front of the house and went in to assure himself that his oil painting *Crossing the Brook* had been properly hung. It was one of the three pictures he was exhibiting at that year's exhibition. Then, as he walked through Bow Street to Oxford Street, observing the street scene around him, it seemed to him, thinking about the painting, that he may have given away too much of himself and his daughters in the picture. Of course, from an artistic point of view there was not much that could be criticized, and the diffuse clarity of the light, the bridge in the middle ground and the surrounding trees were very well represented. Yet the scene might be easy to decode, and the viewer would see that he, Turner, stood in a special relationship to the girls who were crossing. One could sense that Evelina, who had crossed the brook, had become a woman, and that Georgianna, still on the farther bank, was yet a child at the beginning of puberty.

But perhaps he was too sensitive, and people would view the image as the allegory he intended and would see that the chasm before which Evelina finds herself was a symbol for the narrow path from the familiar present to a still unknown and dark future, the veil and the temptation of the unknown.

Impatient, Turner hastened his pace, and when he reached Oxford Street, despite his usual caution about money, he decided to take a coach again in order to more quickly reach his studio and gallery in Harley Street.

Some months ago, a gentleman from Germany, who was interested in landscape painting, had announced he would be in London and requested the pleasure of a visit. Turner had recommended an inn near his studio in Harley Street for the duration of his stay and had invited him to dinner that day. His father very probably was already preparing it. He had also offered the German the possibility of viewing the paintings in his gallery. As a matter of fact, the painter and his father no longer lived in Harley street, having acquired a house called Sandycombe Lodge upstream on the Thames. Today, however, he had wanted the meal served in his gallery so that his visitor would have adequate time to study his paintings.

CHAPTER 2

In his room on the second floor of the inn 'The Old Bell' near Harley Street, Christian August Silberschlag was preparing for his visit with the famous English landscape painter Joseph Mallord William Turner.

The young man was the grandson of the multi-talented Johann Esaias Silberschlag, royal Prussian Consistory Councilor and Head of the Prussian Building Commission, and as such a Privy Councilor, preacher at the Trinity Church in Berlin, headmaster of the Realschule of Berlin, Member of the Berlin Academy of Sciences, the Royal Holland Society of Sciences and Humanities, the Learned Society at Frankfurt on the Oder river and the Berlin Research Society.

This grandfather, who had died in 1791 in peace with God and men, was held very much in honor by his grandson. Christian had been awed by his astounding career and deeply grateful to him for providing for a large part of his education, first at the Royal Realschule in Berlin and then at the Frederick University at Halle, where he studied theology, medicine and mathematics. He had also been given the chance to develop his talent in drawing and painting through private lessons financed by the money his grandfather had left him.

And there was an additional reason why he had loved his grandfather. His father, August Esaias Silberschlag, a member of the Consistory in Magdeburg, who had only recently departed, had been a strict and unforgiving educator, who followed Proverbs 13,24: 'He that spareth his rod hateth his son: but he that loveth him chasteneth him betimes.' Christian had lived in fear of him and had easily broken into tears. His father had tried to cure the boy's sensitive nature through additional harshness.

Therefore, it was like redemption for Christian when he was allowed to join his mild and just grandfather in Berlin and live with him and his dear grandmother Katharina Maria while attending Grammar School. Katharina Maria was still alive, and he visited her whenever he could. When his father died, he had shed honest tears because despite the fear and constant indoctrination he was deeply shaken, which he could hardly understand himself.

By a stroke of luck in 1805, at an event in Halle, he came to know Goethe. It happened as follows. Towards the end of the last century the Viennese doctor Franz Joseph Gall had caused a sensation by maintaining he could by means of measuring the human skull recognize and describe the mental and ethical aptitudes of a human being. He undertook a lecture tour through Germany, which led him to Halle. Goethe was very much interested in this field. When Gall began his lectures in the hall of the 'Crown Prince of Prussia' inn at the Kleine Klausstrasse, he found among his listeners the famous poet and statesman, who had been summoned by the philologist Friedrich August Wolf, Silberschlag's academic teacher. Also, among the crowd, of which half were students from the university, was Silberschlag, whom Wolf introduced to Goethe.

Dr. Gall, surrounded by human and animal skulls as well as wax impressions of brains, did not hesitate to demonstrate his scientific findings by resorting to the heads of some of the prominent guests present. Goethe's skull, he pointed out, was an example of a particularly beautiful and harmonious head which signified an all-round development of the faculties.

Goethe found this interesting and also very entertaining.

Later, though, referring to Gall's phrenology, he asserted that for assessing a person's talents and abilities, brain anatomy and research on brain development was probably more important than examining the structure of the skull.

Still in Halle Goethe fell ill of a disease of the kidneys, for which he consulted the famous professor of medicine Johann Christian Reil. Reil proved himself worthy of his reputation when after having examined Goethe, he did nothing but allow nature to exercise its healing power. This promptly led to Goethe's recovery. During his illness he stayed in Wolf's house in Maerkerstrasse, where Christian August Silberschlag was a regular member at the dinner table through which Professor Wolf attempted to improve his meager professorial salary by offering meals at modest prices.

It was here that Silberschlag came to be of service to the ill genius. In the mornings he removed Goethe's bedpan with nose turned deferentially aside, and he waited on Goethe when he took his meals lying in bed. Also, he was allowed to read to Goethe and show him his attempts at drawing and painting. One evening the poet asked the young man to sit beside his bed and said:

'You will not be surprised, dear Silberschlag, that I have been observing you a little bit during the days of our acquaintanceship. My knowledge of human nature tells me that you have talents above the ordinary. Without doubt your gifts are in the field of the artistic and not so much in what you are trying to do here at Halle university. In fact, you should go on trying your hand at painting. And here you need and are deserving of promotion.'

At such praise Silberschlag blushed, as he stood there in his knickerbockers, black stockings and low shoes, the shirt collar over his jacket, and said:

'Your Excellency is too good to me. You are giving expression to what I have felt sometimes myself, namely that I am not on the right path here at Halle. All the more so as the classical languages are less to my liking than the modern ones, particularly English, which I have had the chance to begin learning with the help of the excellent Master Koch, in fact a classical scholar but fluent in English and familiar with everything related to it.'

Goethe deliberated for a while and then said: 'What, Silberschlag, are the financial means at your disposal?'

'I inherited enough from my grandfather to be independent for the coming years.'

'Then I will make you the following proposal. You accompany me to Weimar, and there at the Free Drawing School you can study and develop your talent under the guidance of my good friend, the painter and art critic Johann Heinrich Meyer. At the same time, I will take care that you can perfect your English in the house of Charles Gore and his daughters Eliza and Emily. And for all this, dear friend, you will help me to order my collection of paintings and drawings in my house on the Frauenplan and put them into a decent catalog.'

And so it came about that Silberschlag moved to Weimar, settled there for a few years, continued learning English, assisted the genius organizing his collections without daring to charge him anything, and at the same time was able to acquire an artistic education and a more refined taste through his social intercourse with Goethe, his friend Heinrich Meyer and the rest of the Weimar society, which was deeply involved in all matters of art. His talent for creative painting and drawing, however, soon proved to be limited, though he was found to have considerable inclination and skill for copying the works of others.

In September of the year 1810 Silberschlag accompanied Goethe on a trip to Dresden, where they visited the workshop of the painter Caspar David Friedrich, situated near the Elbe river. There when he saw the paintings *The Abbey in the Oakwood* and *The Monk by the Sea*, it came to him as a revelation that this was what painting should be. When the others departed the workshop, he stayed behind, got into conversation with the painter and became quite enthused by the artist's dark, lonesome and melancholic disposition with its transcendental longing for the Beyond. Friedrich too liked the young man and they renewed their friendship one year later when they met during an outing to the Lobdeburg castle near Jena that had been undertaken by Goethe with friends and acquaintances.

Friedrich invited Silberschlag to come to Dresden again and see the fascinating landscape, the varied surroundings, the splendid baroque architecture, the academy, galleries and studios as well as meet an enlightened society and experience the vivid tourist traffic. The difference to Weimar was distinct, because despite all the geniuses present, the latter remained a smallish provincial place. And so Silberschlag, whom Goethe was not unwilling to let go after the work on his collections was completed, came to Dresden. Here he lived on what he had inherited and from what he earned through private English lessons, which had come into fashion again when Napoleon's end became imminent. Though Saxony and particularly Dresden had, without hesitation and unnecessary patriotic sentiments, enjoyed Napoleon's favor and had warmed themselves in his imperial sun, the people soon realized which side their bread was buttered on and turned to the new or rather old powers, namely Prussia, Austria, England and Russia.

Silberschlag often visited Friedrich in his poorly equipped flat and obtained a thorough insight into his work and the world of his thought. Talks with the painter Kuegelgen and the physician Carus, who was also a painter, about Friedrich provided him with additional insights as well.

Soon after he had settled down, he got to know the nineteen-year-old Johanna, a delicate but at the same time resolute maiden, daughter of the grocer Bergling in Bautzener Strasse in Dresden-Neustadt. At first Silberschlag could hardly believe that the Neustadt could be home to such a graceful and at the same time mysterious flower of a girl.

Johanna was of medium height, had chestnut hair, large brown eyes and a beautiful alto voice.

Her figure, which Silberschlag soon had the opportunity to research in more detail, was slim but sturdy, and her summer dress could hardly hide her beautiful legs and the sweetest little bosom a man could wish for.

Johanna's father was quite willing to let Silberschlag woo his daughter when he discovered that this possible son-in-law associated with quite respectable circles.

So it did not take long for the two young people to be engaged and then, after the proper time, to be married and to move in with Johanna's parents, who had a large house in Bautzener Strasse and a roomy flat on the second floor, which they hoped would soon see the play of a grandchild.

And Goethe had not forgotten Silberschlag. In the year 1815 the painter and architect Karl Friedrich Schinkel was commissioned by his King to buy at tolerable prices good English land- and seascapes for a new museum. He asked Goethe if he could recommend a reliable and knowledgeable person who he could send to England. Goethe thought of Silberschlag, who now knew much about painting and could speak English well. So Silberschlag was tasked with the honorable job of traveling to England and seek out exemplary works among the famous landscape painters.

In his room in 'The Old Bell', Silberschlag could hardly believe how fortune and coincidence had brought him here. He had traveled to Berlin to meet Schinkel after a tearful—on both sides—farewell and a promise to Johanna that she would get letters from him as often as possible. She on the other hand said she would use his absence in order to complete their household and improve her knowledge of art and music, about which she already had become quite cognizant.

In Berlin he got his instructions and a generous traveling fund from the royal extraordinario, the King's purse for special expenditures.

Schinkel would have liked to go himself, but his work in the Prussian Building Commission took most of his time. Additionally, Chancellor Carl August Fürst von Hardenberg had entrusted him with the task of purchasing a certain collection of pictures in the Rhineland. In addition, he could not speak English.

Initially, Silberschlag was not to buy pictures but to first get an impression of the state of landscape painting in England. What he could do was to acquire options on pictures he thought would be acceptable to the King's new museum.

In preparation of all that and also in order to answer questions his hosts in England might put to him about the state of the art in Germany he had carefully studied the works of the new romantic landscape painters. Thus, he felt well equipped for his job, particularly by his intimate knowledge of the works of his friend Caspar David Friedrich.

So, he had arrived in London that autumn.

'The Old Bell', where for a few days he had now resided, had been built in the last third of the 17th century. At first it had served as accommodation and eating place for the workers rebuilding that part of London after the great fire of 1666.

It became for Silberschlag a real home to which he could escape from the sometimes disquieting giant London and its penetrating and moist autumn coldness.

CHAPTER 3

London, November 17th in the year of 1815.

My dearest and most loved Johanna!

Merchant Moser's clerk has just left me after delivering your most desired letter of November 10th. So quickly did Moser and his clerk and servant make the journey to London from Dresden that it reached me in a mere 18 days. Their trip across the channel, they said, had been greatly aided by a favorable wind. I gave the clerk a good tip and asked him to thank Herr Moser in your and my names. Also he should be kind enough to drop by before returning to Germany, expected to happen on the 25th of November to pick up my letters to you, as well as to Privy Councilor Schinkel and His Excellency Goethe.

Dearest Johanna, my longing for you and your caresses is growing daily, and the great distance between us and the lengthening time of separation really speak of how you have become a part of me and the center of my life. But have patience, I say to my heart; new experiences and little adventures can perhaps prove good for our love.

Your loving letter has warmed my heart and very much increased my joyful anticipation of our reunion in beautiful Dresden. I thank you for the greetings that your dear parents as well as my dear Friedrich and the gentlemen Carus and Kügelgen have asked you to include. Thank them very much and give them my deeply felt greetings. There will be much to tell when I am back, because time and paper would not suffice to put everything into a letter.

But now I want to report to you what it is like in this London. Please save my letters carefully because they are to serve as part of my travel report and act as a diary.

My love, having come from Weimar, and living in Dresden, I thought I knew what a big city, a real Grossstadt, is like.

Truly naive this seems to me today.

What I am experiencing here surpasses, no, overwhelms all my expectations. The city in its size, stateliness and power is incomparable.

It is the hub of the Empire. It is also the center of the world's economy, a role it has taken over from Amsterdam. London's great wealth stems from the trade with East and West India and the two Americas, in fact with all parts of the world. It leads in the spheres of literature, theater and the arts. Here live the most famous painters and architects, manufacturers of valuable furniture and renowned gold and silver smiths. There are banks and factories and the incomparable harbor.

More than two million people live and work in London. If one compares that to the number of our dear Dresdeners, which, as you know, has recently reached 57,000, our population seems almost insignificant. One hardly dares remember that since the unhappy alliance of our King with Napoleon, there are only 1 million and 183 thousand subjects remaining in Saxony, that is to say fewer inhabitants than in the city of London.

London. Incalculable alone is the number of wagons and ships which supply the city with the coal, the wood, the building materials for the houses, the food for the large population, the raw materials for the factories, the pulp wood for the manufacture of the paper for the many newspapers and printing shops, the valuables and delicacies from distant continents for the households of the well-to-do, and all the things a great city requires. Day and night, year in year out, without interruption. My dearest treasure, when I come to think of Dresden now, it appears to me to be a bright Arcadia, sunny, peaceful and serene.

Nevertheless, I have started to like London. During the time I have been here I have looked around and talked to people of the most varied levels of society. Some I have met in the galleries and museums, others in pubs, in shops and in the streets.

In particular I feel drawn to the colorful life of the East End. Here I've become quickly accustomed to the London way of speaking and begin to understand the people more easily and am able to express myself fairly well.

It is now that I realize for the first time how important proper pronunciation is, which Master Koch at Halle took so much trouble to teach us. It really helps me to get along with the Londoners and they seem to appreciate my efforts. I have even become familiar with the language of the Cockneys, though I would not dare imitate them. Cockneys are those Londoners who are born within earshot of the bells of St.

Mary-le-Bow in the Cheapside district of London. These people are more hospitable, tolerant and talkative than I had expected, and their innocence somewhat reminds me of the Dresdeners.

In Whitechapel, a district in London's east side with its sugar boiling plants, iron foundries, oilcloth factories, clothing industries and many others it seemed to me as if the streets are a garish mosaic of the wider world. Jews with black ringlets, beards, kippahs and side curls, almond-eyed women in phantasmagoric saris, Chinamen with short pigtails and pointed hats, black sailors—in short, people from all over the world walk the streets, visit the inns and regard the city as their home.

Now, my dearest Johanna, I must confess something to you, and only to you. In my desire to research everything and to get to know land and customs thoroughly, all in order to be able to tell you as much and as truthfully as possible, the day before yesterday my curiosity got the better of me and drove me to follow a pretty young woman, who had addressed me, up to the entrance of a public house. Here of course I remembered my love for you and stopped. I also thought that the King's money in my traveling fund was not intended to be used for the services of this person, not even if it was only to relieve my loneliness for a while.

When she noticed that I did not follow her into the house, she quickly shed her inviting manner and became nothing less than a fury, screaming and causing a veritable commotion at which the passersby stopped and stared at me. I fled the site in an unworthy haste and decided to let this experience be a useful lesson.

Back to the city. In all this, I was not so awed as to overlook a quite different London that exists as well. This is the city of the poor, the vulnerable, the criminals and the outcasts. Elderly people told me about Tyburn, a truly frightening place. As late as the last decades of the past century the name played a gruesome role in the lives of the city and the people. It was repulsive and at the same time incited a sensational lust among the crowds. Originally Tyburn was the name of a small river which crossed London from the heights of Hampstead through Regent's Park down to the low land of Westminster, where it flowed into the swampy flood area of the Thames south of Green Park. Its two arms formed the small gravel island of Westminster. From the 13th century onwards it supplied London with water, which flowed through elm wood pipes to tapping points in the city or directly to the houses and palaces of the rich.

You know, my sweetheart, what my grandfather in Berlin had told me about the grandiosity of Roman brick-lined fresh water conduits and sewage tunnels, the remains of which can still be seen in Cologne, Trier and Bath. He also spoke of the deplorable state of the medieval and even modern water supply in the big cities in Europe, be it in Dresden, Berlin or even here in London.

Here I quite conscientiously inquired about the state of water supply and waste water disposal (and I am sure Privy Councilor Schinkel will be very interested to hear about it) and found that the unclean conditions here too again and again have led to outbreaks of dangerous illnesses, epidemics, and plagues.

But this was not what stirred my imagination. Rather it was the fact that Tyburn acquired notoriety for the gallows of Middlesex, which stood west of the river at the north-east end of Hyde Park. From the 13th century onward it was the main place of execution in London, though not the only one.

In Tyburn, murderers and robbers were hanged, often after being wheeled most savagely in front of the spectators, who watched enthusiastically from grandstands specially erected for this purpose.

'What is he that builds stronger than either the mason, the shipwright or the carpenter? The gallows-maker, for that frame outlives a thousand tenants.'

Do you still remember when we were reading *Hamlet* together how we were amused and yet wondered about this curiosity? This can really be called a conundrum and is still popular in ale houses.

The Tower on the other hand was the place where traitors and members of the royal family and high nobility were beheaded. The execution site in Wapping was used for pirates, though all these distinctions were not always observed properly, which says something about the insufficient orderliness of the English.

Only a few years ago, namely in 1783, the practice in Tyburn was ended, while executions as such are still taking place, everywhere. You remember when the case of the alleged child murderess Johanna Catharina Hoehn was to be decided, even our venerated Excellency Goethe in his capacity as member of the Privy Council in Weimar voted in a way that did not help to prevent the execution of the poor woman.

Dearest, please excuse my letter for being somewhat higgledy-piggledy, but my heart is so full that I cannot at the moment bring more order to the excess of impressions, and thoughts I am experiencing.

The abyss which opens here between the glamour of the palaces and churches and residences and businesses in Westminster and the miserable flats and streets and alleyways frightens me and sometimes leaves me bewildered. Should that be the God-given course of the world?

The houses are small and narrow, and the streets are sometimes just 15 feet wide. Officially it is said that the overcrowding of the houses is caused by the poor, lazy, negligent and dirty folks themselves. And the factories, which are to be found everywhere, are also dirty and smelly. Dye works and chemical factories, fertilizer and soot black manufacturers, glue, paraffin, dye and bone-meal factories all pollute air and water and make people prematurely sick and invalid. The East End, people say, has become an abyss, a netherworld, a world of strange secrets and desires. It is the part of London in which more poor people are living in grossly overcrowded houses than in the rest of London combined, and from this concentrated poverty can be heard tales of evil and vice, of cruelties and unspeakable crimes.

The Ratcliffe Highway murders of just four years ago are fresh in memory and show that this area represents the most chaotic and dangerous part of the city.

I asked my landlord to tell me this story in detail. Four people and a child were killed in Ratcliffe Highway No. 29, and in 'The King's Arms' in Old Gravel Lane, all near Wapping, a publican, his wife and their maid were put to death. No one could provide a motive for these seven murders. John Williams alias John Murphy, an Irish or Scottish sailor, was finally accused. In the night before his threatening arrest he hanged himself. Someone, to prevent his returning as an undead, hammered a stake through his heart before he was buried where the New Road is intersected by Cannon Street Road. Who knows if not some day his remains together with the stake in his chest will be found in order to confirm to later generations the truth of these events? My publican warned me urgently not to walk this area alone late in the evening or even at night.

In contrast, our lives in Dresden, my darling, despite the travails that everybody has to live with, seems peaceful and safe, though I admit that with the modest assets we own and my other income we belong to the privileged.

Now I am coming to something that can break one's very heart, especially if one, like ourselves, is hoping to be richly blessed with children. (Tell me, my love, are you feeling anything stir under your heart yet?)

A beadle, which is what a communal servant is called here, who the publican introduced me to in a tavern, told me some stories which robbed me of sleep for some nights. The beadle's tongue had been loosened by several half-pints, as the usual glass of beer is called here and roughly corresponds to a quarter of a liter. I had been wondering about some unusual names which can be heard quite frequently, and the beadle told me that foundlings are often named after the place where they had been picked up. For example, names such as Peter Piazza, Mary Piazza and Paul Piazza for Covent Garden are not rare. 'Children abandoned in the streets', as they are called, are a good reason for the beadles to celebrate. As is well known they are given ten pounds for every child they take charge of. And because the children do not often survive very long in their care, the beadles can soon spend the money for a small celebration. That's why, I fear, my beadle was in such a good and talkative mood

Of course, the chap declined all responsibility for the circumstances that lead to such deadly outcomes. He admitted that he had heard of a parish in Westminster where out of 500 foundlings only one child survived. Should they survive they are accommodated in workhouses, which resemble small and simple factories. There they work from six in the morning to six at night. They spin wool or flax or knit socks. My beadle emphasized that one hour per day is granted for learning and one for eating and playing. After all, he said, one must not forget that children by their very nature are evil like small, untamed wild animals and must be locked up and tamed by discipline and punishment. The master to whom they are sold after their time in the workhouse can do with them what he thinks right. For example, he can use the girls for his pleasure, and, if they do not obey him in this or in all other things, he can let them go hungry.

Perhaps it will not surprise you, my dear, that I am planning after my return to you and the joys awaiting me, to look around in Dresden more thoroughly and research, above all, the life of the poorer classes in order not to pass too unjust a judgment on London. We know that one often does not see what lies before one's eyes while as a visitor one regards things with a sharper vision. (The joys I am referring to and the details of which I often think about help me endure our separation).

By the way, the engravings of a certain William Hogarth, painter, engraver and satirist, whose work is well-known and much sought after in England, have furthered my insights significantly even though he has been dead for fifty years. I bought some of his engravings on my own account, hoping, of course, that I can sell them in Dresden with some profit. We will look at them together.

What I like best are Hogarth's serial genre pictures, mostly done in oil and later reproduced as copperplates. They show political and social evils. Even if the painter was attacking the conditions of seventy years ago in his painted satires, I must say that things are not much different now, neither in the poor- and workhouses nor in the prisons and foundling houses. But it comforts me a little that people are at least made aware of what is going on around them. That is, to my mind, the precondition for a betterment.

I am quite determined to inform our friend Friedrich about my experiences in detail in order to arouse his interest in such themes, which will not be easy seeing what he is most inclined to treat in his work.

Moreover, I think I will try to bring up Hogarth's pictures when I talk to Mr. Turner, which will happen presently, in order to learn what he thinks about him. Naturally I must tread carefully here, because experience has taught me that nothing causes an artist to fall into a cold silence more quickly than laudatory words about another artist. You remember that I told you once what a cool atmosphere arose when in a conversation with Excellency Goethe, I quoted a few verses from Schiller which I had liked.

With this I must close my letter, because something quite special is waiting for me, namely the mentioned visit with Professor Turner.

Give my best wishes to all who remember me and be assured that I remain as ever and eternally yours Silberschlag.

He put the quill down, spread sand on the letter to dry the ink, folded, sealed and addressed it.

He took the poker, pushed the coal to a little heap in the fireplace, piled ash on it to keep the ember so that it would still be warm when he returned from Turner's studio. It was not easy to stop thinking of Johanna and to leave so cozy and warm a room for the gray and foggy November chill that awaited him outside. On the other hand, he was looking forward to dinner with Professor Turner. He had tasted many a dish in the various eating establishments in London, and was quite eager to learn what his host would offer him in his house.

He was also somewhat apprehensive, now that he would soon meet the famous painter. He hoped he would be able to converse in a way that would satisfy the outstanding artist.

It did not help that he had heard rumors in London that the man was, if not becoming unhinged, at least suffering from some disease of the eyes. No longer, it was whispered, were objects depicted as such in his pictures, as befits decent paintings, but were mere proper visions. It was as if all the glow and magic of the sun had descended and threatened to drown the observer in them, from a fabulous wild orange, shimmering blue, opalescent green, bloody scarlet, screaming yellow, silvery iridescent gray, grim hellish black to sparkling gold.

Since the year 1802 Turner had, as Silberschlag knew, been a member of the Royal Academy, and since 1807 had pursued his great plan of publishing his *Liber studiorum*, a series of 100 prints with which he desired to convey to posterity the great diversity and the vast extent of his work. *Liber studiorum* was intended to be an expression of his fundamental beliefs regarding the art of landscape painting. The work categorized the genre into six types: Marine, Mountainous, Pastoral, Historical, Architectural, and Elevated or Epic Pastoral. It also included cityscapes and seascapes, the latter mainly included paintings of ships, shipwrecks and shore scenes.

Turner, so Silberschlag had heard during his visits to galleries and exhibitions in London, was said to be shy, particularly when the person he was meeting was shy or insecure as well, a tendency perhaps caused by his small stature. On the other hand, he could be direct and brusque, which could be quite intimidating. Silberschlag resolved to present himself in a manner polite and respectful, but to avoid any appearance of submissiveness.

He put on a hat and a thick overcoat, used thumb and forefinger to put out the tallow candle on his table, threw a longing glance at the warm fireplace, then took his umbrella from the stand by the door and left the room. He went down the stairs, crossed through the pub full of pipe smoke and beer haze greeting the publican behind the counter, and stepped out onto the street.

CHAPTER 4

Turner alighted from the coach in front of his gallery in Queen Anne Street, paid the coachman and entered the house.

Originally the entrance had been in Harley Street. But as he had wished to strengthen his independence as a painter and his position in the academy after some quarrels, he had purchased the property directly behind his house and had it converted to a gallery. Now one entered the house from Queen Anne Street running at a right angle to Harley Street.

He was in a good mood and was looking forward to dinner with his guest and to the showing of his work. And also, of course, to a conversation about English and German painting. Normally he was rather disinclined to let anybody come too near him. And his father, who watched almost jealously over his welfare and his artistic career, was careful not to let people molest him. But the visitor today was an exception. He came from Germany, and the painter hoped not only to gather information about painting in that country but also about the land itself. His journey to the continent in 1802 had taken him to France and Switzerland. More than 400 drawings resulted and they were to serve him for years, as he painted pictures from scenes that had particularly impressed him. But Germany, beautiful, troubled, mythical and many times divided, still remained unseen by him.

Tonight, he would hear something about German painting and would pass on his own views. This he liked to do because he wanted people to understand that painting was more than just the vain reflection of the artist in his work. Painting, or writing for that matter, rather showed in a very individual, subjective way how he saw the world and wanted his viewers or readers to see it.

Turner took the big front-door key from his pocket, cleaned his boots on the scraper, opened the door and entered the house. He called for his father, who responded immediately. The older man came down the stairs, took his son's hat and helped him out of his coat.

Turner said, 'Here are the rent takings, Father. As usual with the Buckle family I had to wait quite a while before they could scrape the money together. And they still have two outstanding payments, but I can't bring myself to have them evicted. The man almost works himself to death on the docks, and the woman suffers from consumption. And the children are so skinny and pale, you can hardly look at them. They have already sold a boy to a chimney sweeper, and now they are waiting for the second oldest to reach the age of five so that they can sell him too.'

Turner's father took the money and secured it in an oak chest, iron-bound and provided with padlocks, which stood behind a curtain in a recess of the hall. Then he said, 'You shouldn't take this to heart too much. And above all you mustn't let the lives of the paupers interfere with your painting and reduce its attraction to certain customers. After all, they don't want to see in pictures what they try to avoid seeing daily in the streets. Your paintings sell so well because they depict the world in its wildness, its overwhelming beauty and its poetry.

There are the well-to-do and the poor, as God created them, and we should be content with it and be happy to belong to the former.

Go and get yourself warm. The meal is on the fire, the table is laid and our guest may soon come.'

As Turner went up the stairs his father watched him affectionately. He knew that his son had been at a brothel again that day, but he was prepared to excuse the habit, as he excused almost everything his son had done since he began selling the twelve-year-old boy's drawings in his barber and wig-maker's shop for three shillings.

Naturally at that time he had hoped William would eventually take over the business from him. But imagine the loss to the world if his son had become a wig-maker instead of the famous painter.

When William was fourteen, he had been lucky to escape the narrow streets of Covent Garden in London. In the summer of 1789, the young artist stayed at Sunningwell, near Oxford, with his maternal uncle Joseph Marshall, and he roamed the countryside and filled a sketchbook with pencil drawings of buildings and views in and around Oxford, from some of which he made watercolors.

This uncle was well-disposed towards him, and had taken care of him previously when in the year of '83 his only surviving sibling, his sister Mary Ann, died and the eight-year-old boy suffered a nervous breakdown. At that time his uncle was a butcher in Brentford, a small market town ten miles from London. Later the boy attended John White's school there and in his leisure time came to know a Thames river quite different from the one in London. In Brentford, it meandered through an idyllic landscape and strongly influenced the young man and his future as a painter.

As soon as his son had established his own household, his father assumed the part of the homemaker and oversaw all domestic concerns.

Soon he was able to enjoy William's first success, when a painting was selected by the Royal Academy for its yearly exhibition of 1790. This was a watercolor of the archbishop of Canterbury's palace at Lambeth. The work was not sold, and after the exhibition his son generously gave it to his father, who presented it to his friend John Narraway of Bristol.

From then on, he completely devoted himself to his son so that he could pursue his art and his other needs undisturbed. He became his servant, studio assistant and secretary.

He prepared the canvasses and did the priming; he went shopping and managed the money. He felt that his son, because of the instability and hysteria of his mother, had had a difficult early life, and in consequence, despite a strong sensuality, had decided as a man to remain a bachelor.

Turner's mother, Mary Marshall, who was six years older than her husband, was often morose and prone to destructive fits of rage. In the end she was judged insane and she died in an asylum in 1804. The older Turner reproached himself for having exposed his son to such early sorrows and now did everything in his power to serve in the place of the absent mother and wife.

As he reflected on this, there came a knock on the door. He went and opened it and before him stood their guest with the umbrella in one hand and his hat in the other.

'Come in, my dear. William is expecting you,' he said. After taking Silberschlag's hat, coat and umbrella he led him up the stairs, which ended on a landing, on which a small table and a chair could be seen. Two doors came into sight, and even before the old Turner could knock one of them opened and the painter stepped into the opening. At first Silberschlag could only see the contours of a small, stocky man, because the room behind him was brilliantly lit and dazzled him. Turner, approaching him and grasping his hand, looked up at him, though Silberschlag himself was only of medium height.

He said, 'Welcome to my gallery. I can easily imagine what it must feel like here in London for somebody coming from Germany, especially in autumn with this foggy weather.'

At this moment Silberschlag could not but remember a cartoon which made fun of Turner, depicting him as a dwarf with a big top-hat on his head. The Turner in the picture swung a kind of mop, which he held like a lance and from which yellow paint was dripping, which in the next moment he would smear on the canvas standing ready before him. This picture expressed undoubtedly what many of his contemporaries were thinking, namely that Turner was not quite right in his head and painted with soap suds and whitewash. Silberschlag had read somewhere that Turner measured only 5 feet and 4 inches in height, which in Germany, as he would write his Johanna, corresponded to 1.63 cm, based on the metric system the French had introduced in 1799. He felt a bit guilty for recalling such disrespectful parodies and therefore made a deeper bow than was usual. He allowed himself be drawn into the room and answered:

'Many thanks, Professor Turner, for receiving me.'

Seeing the deep bow and hearing the word professor, Turner was surprised to be greeted like this. What did it mean in a more or less private meeting? Did his guest allow himself a certain liberty? Did he want to make fun of him? But this would not be in keeping with what Turner knew about the Germans. He continued looking at Silberschlag without letting go of his hand. The latter began to feel uneasy; had he made a mistake? Or was this part of the eccentricity he had heard rumored about the painter?

But Turner's thoughts were suddenly somewhere else. They went back to the year 1807, when he was appointed professor. After this elevation several years passed before he started his lectures on perspective. The preparation went on endlessly, because the subject not only concerned the rules of linear perspective but included all possible problems of spatial perspective. An important aspect dealt with what had come to be called air perspective, which was founded on Leonardo's observation that distant objects in a landscape appear bluish through the turbidity of the atmosphere. Moreover, when preparing his lectures, he put much stress on answering the question of how the background of a scene should be painted. He had already questioned the traditional rules of perspective in his own art and therefore in front of his students dealt only with the fundamental questions. Increasingly, over the course of years a few experts and his father became his real audience, experts who appreciated the illustrations he had made expressly for these lectures. And with these Turner felt growing unease, feeling a need to bypass most of the rules of perspective in favor of the effect of pure color.

Suddenly he realized that he was still holding the hand of his visitor and so causing him embarrassment. Therefore, drawing him further into the gallery, he let go of his hand and, to make amends for his absent-mindedness, said in a particularly friendly way:

'Dear friend, please feel quite at home in my house.'

Silberschlag at once felt a certain nearness, a degree of familiarity which did not occur so quickly with other nationalities, especially not with his own compatriots. He had experienced this once before in Weimar, when he had visited Charles Gore and his daughters Eliza and Emily. The English—could he already say that after his limited experience so far? —had a special talent for putting their vis-a-vis in a pleasant and relaxed mood. Without many words they made one feel as an equal.

This was much to Silberschlag's liking, as his father had spared no effort in imparting in him a feeling of inferiority, which had led to a shyness and inhibition towards people who were self-confident and determined.

Happily, he had, through reflection, been careful to avoid the mistake some of his compatriots were prone to, particularly when they sat comfortably in an ale house with their beer. This happened when they mistook the friendliness the English exhibited for a desire for a quick familiarity, which often led to the unpleasant surprise of being snubbed for assuming a premature intimacy.

Ceasing his ruminations, he decided to open himself to the hospitable atmosphere which his host had created with his words.

The room in which they now found themselves was of considerable size, measuring about 70 by 30 feet. The windows opened to the south-west so that, whatever the time of the day, the season, or the weather in London sufficient light was available for viewing the paintings.

The walls were whitewashed in order to increase the effect of the light. The floor was made of oak boards, smoothly planed and waxed. Everywhere, on ledges on the walls, on small tables and shelves, on window sills and wherever there was space available, tallow candles stood. There were also lamps with which Silberschlag was unfamiliar. He asked his host to allow him a closer look. Turner beckoned him to come nearer and said:

'This is in my eyes the first real innovation in oil lamps in a thousand years. We can thank the Swiss inventor Aimè Argand, who had them patented here in England about thirty years ago. Believe me, without these lamps I could have painted only half of what I have so far considering the light conditions in London.'

He took a lamp, turned the wick down so that the lamp went out, and continued:

'See here the wick? I remove the glass cylinder—please hand me the cloth from over there—it is still very hot. This cylinder serves to increase the air draft. And now, do you see the cylindrical wick between the two concentric metal tubes?'

Silberschlag, who had inherited from his grandfather an interest in all things technical, responded:

'Allow me to try to find out the principle according to which this lamp works. Obviously, the inner tube allows the air to flow through the center and support the burning of the oil at the inner surface of the cylindrical flame. And this happens in addition to the combustion at the outer surface. Simply ingenious.'

'Yes,' replied Turner, 'this you can say. The lamp emits ten times more light than the earlier lamps of the same size, though it needs more oil, but actually less if you consider its efficiency. So, to say it again, the light is much brighter than a candle, burns cleanly, and is cheaper than using candles.'

Turning the wick up again, he took a tallow candle, relit the lamp and replaced the glass cylinder.

Now in the bright light Silberschlag saw the painting before which the lamp had been placed. Turner, however noticing Silberschlag's glance, said:

'Oh, no, my friend. The pictures can wait. Dinner comes first. And there is my father already.'

Turner's father had indeed entered through the door and was fetching a large cast-iron pot he called a stockpot, from the grate over the fire.. This he placed on a big round table, which had been pushed near the fireplace. Silberschlag did not know the word stockpot and immediately decided to include it into his vocabulary.

The wine glasses had already been filled.

'I hope you will like my meal. It is Scotch Broth. Some might be inclined to call it, wrongly I think, a pauper's meal. My son brought the recipe from his first trip to Scotland fourteen years ago. Yes, I remember, it was in 1801.'

Silberschlag, when he saw the pot and the plate with bread, which old Turner now added to the dishes on the table, wondered if this was the dinner he had been looking forward to so curiously? He must wait and see what the stockpot would offer. There need not always be several courses in a meal, he told himself. He looked with interest at what the old man ladled on his plate. The steaming broth looked rather colored. When all the plates were filled, Turner raised his glass to his father and their guest and everybody drank. Then they started eating without any grace being said.

The candles and lamps and the open fire had warmed the gallery in a most agreeable way. Together with the brightness of the wide room, the unexpected friendliness of his hosts, the fine meal and the promise of viewing the paintings, all put Silberschlag in a pleasant and dreamy state and caused him to forget for a while the clammy cold of the London autumn. He felt the warmth loosen his limbs and heighten his good mood.

'Before you waste time finding out what exactly my father put on our plates, I will tell you how this recipe came to our notice.'

Silberschlag, who had found the first spoonfuls of the broth very tasty, nodded expectantly.

'I'll mention first that for me a good meal should whenever possible be connected to a reminiscence, to a fragrance, to the joy of a first encounter, the recollection of the atmosphere and the meal's history. This helps to raise the meal above the mere appeasement of one's hunger and makes it part of our culture, which elevates us above the animals and from which our mind is nourished even before our body.'

Silberschlag agreed. 'Yes, you are completely right. In my time in Weimar I found that Excellency Goethe always held a good dinner in high esteem. It was remarkable how he increased the importance of the midday meal by neglecting breakfast and supper. Thus, he made the main meal a little cultural climax of the day. In the mornings he used to take alternatively tea, chocolate or bouillon. In the evenings he did not eat at all but just had a cup of tea or some wine. In this he was encouraged by the macrobiotics of the famous Hufeland, who in his book ...'

Here Silberschlag broke off abruptly because it occurred to him that he had talked too long and perhaps had given the impression that he wanted to boast of his close acquaintance with Goethe.

But Turner, father and son, had listened attentively. Then the father said:

'Quite interesting, how habits and traditions differ. I would never let my son leave home in the mornings without first having fed him with a substantial breakfast. And this breakfast usually is back bacon, poached eggs, grilled tomatoes, fried mushrooms, black pudding, baked beans, smoked trout and toasted bread with butter. You can imagine that together with several mugs of tea this breakfast sees William through most of the day, though for a short time after breakfast he sometimes does feel a bit dizzy, as he has confessed.'

During this talk all three of them had busily used their spoons availing themselves as well of the bread and the wine.

'Now,' Turner said, 'let me say something about this Scotch Broth that my father has so lovingly and tastefully prepared and that I have appointed one of our main dishes.'

Here Silberschlag nodded emphatically.

'On my first trip to Scotland about fourteen years ago I accidentally met a family Brown in Crathie on the river Dee. The Browns were farmers, not rich but very hospitable.

It came about one evening, when I had watched the autumnal fogs in the Dee valley and made a number of sketches. A woman from a nearby farm approached me, and introducing herself as Mrs. Brown, asked if I would like to have dinner with them. As it had grown too dark to go on sketching and I had become hungry, I followed her into the house. The kitchen, which served also as the living-room and the bedroom for the children, was warm and cozy. A kettle hung over the fire, on the walls could be seen pots and pans, in the corner beside the door stood broom and dustpan, and to the left of the fire on a layer of straw lay two little lambs, perhaps two weeks old. In front of the fire on an old rug a cat had coiled up and was purring.

Mrs. Brown asked me to sit down at the table, which had already been laid, and said her husband and son would come later. She then served me the meal, which she simply called broth. I ate and in between asked her for the recipe.

"That is easy to remember. Soak two handfuls of peas in water overnight. Then you take a neck of lamb and bring it to the boil in a good amount of water with the peas, a handful of pearl barley, pepper and salt. Skim. Add 1 large cup of diced carrot, 1 large cup of diced turnip, 1 chopped onion and leek. Simmer for one and a half hours, add one quarter of a white cabbage, shredded, and 1 cup of grated carrot. Simmer for half an hour. Before serving, add 1 tablespoon of parsley. Now, how do you like it?"

Meanwhile I had emptied my plate for the second time and said with full heart and stomach, "Thank you, Mrs. Brown. This has been the most excellent meal I have had since leaving London."

My hostess smiled quite happily, but so broadly that it was as if both corners of her mouth had said good-bye to each other for good.

"Now," she said, "you must stay here for a bit to taste our home-brewed beer and meet my husband and above all our son. There is a little mystery attached to the boy, so to say dark and a bit crazy. Old woman Fleming from the other end of the village prophesied something really odd for him or rather my grandson."

Here she lowered her voice though nobody was near who could eavesdrop:

"A son of my son, that is to say my grandson, who has not been born yet but is to be baptized with the name of his father, John, shall one day occupy a special position at the English royal court. Can you imagine such a nonsense?" But she did not look as if she considered this prophesy nonsense. Rather she looked somewhat hopeful.

I said no, I couldn't, but added that in this world strange things do happen. Would, for example, my father, a wig-maker and barber, have dreamed that his son would one day become a well-known painter and a member of the Royal Academy?

Naturally my friendly hostess could not really understand the significance of what I had said, but clearly understood that even simple origins from time to time result in the most astonishing circumstances of life.

'Now, my young friend, how did you like it?'

Silberschlag, whose mind had already drifted to the painting he had only glimpsed before dinner, recalled himself anticipating that they would presently have an interesting exchange of ideas.

'Ah, the meal was quite excellent, Mr. Turner. If this is what poor people eat one would rather be poor. Of course, it must be served really hot, as you have done.' With this he turned to the father. 'Hot it must be so that it keeps body and soul together in the autumn cold of Scotland as well as in the fog of London. It sort of tastes—how shall I call it—'round'. That is what we would say in Germany. The meat imparts to it the required hearty depth and fullness of taste and the vegetables at the same time give it a lighter quality.

I must not miss preparing this for my wife, when I return to Dresden. I like to cook, you know,' he added diffidently. This was a confession he normally made only among very close friends, but here the good and intimate atmosphere had been too tempting to keep silent. From the miens of his hosts he could discern that his remark was more appreciated by the old Turner than the young. The painter very probably would have no time for such trifles.

CHAPTER 5

Turner refilled the wine glasses and remarked:

'By rights we should be drinking a strong ale or even whiskey with this meal and also afterward. But as I know your native country, your *heimat*, produces the best white wines in Europe, which you are certainly accustomed to, we are drinking white wine today.'

He lifted his glass, and drank Silberschlag's health.

The latter joined him in the drink, swirling it around in his mouth to savor the taste and responded:

'For this I am very grateful. It is true, above the Elbe River near Dresden and Meissen they produce an excellent wine. In autumn during grape harvest there is a wonderful view from the heights over the river or in summer one can observe the growth and ripening in the vineyards. And if it becomes too hot—hardly imaginable sitting here—you can descend the Elbe valley, visit one of the wine taverns under the cold rocky walls and enjoy a glass of last year's vintage. If there you also enjoy a freshly caught Elbe trout, then your happiness is complete, at least for the moment.'

Both Turners could not help but smile at the expression of yearning which could be seen on the young man's face, when he mentioned the summer heat in Saxony.

'Don't believe,' the painter said comfortingly, 'that the weather here is always that cold and damp. We have hot summers and warm autumns, too, and as far as I know

London and Dresden are situated on the same geographical latitude. Though I admit grapes for wine would not grow here now, they did, however, in Roman times. But let's go and see the paintings, I can sense your impatience.'

They rose and went first to the painting Silberschlag had only glimpsed before dinner, while father Turner began to clear the table.

Under the painting there was a slip of paper with the name of the work, a text in the form of a poem and more information: *Snow Storm: Hannibal and his army crossing the Alps. Exhibited 1812. Oil on canvas.*

The size of the painting caused Silberschlag to hastily take a step back. It was large, perhaps one and a half by two and a half meters, which did not bear approaching too close. Also, he was struck by an overarching richness of color in the sky and earth that could only exercise its intended effect if viewed from the proper distance. An almost complete spectrum of light was visible like a vast sky-high wave which threatened to smother the tiny men and animals under a crimson veiled sun. Nearness and distance, foreground and background seemed to be equally threatening, and the way to safety indicated by the bright light in the distance could be understood not so much as symbolizing dreamland Italy as the entrance to hell.

'I can't make out Hannibal,' said Silberschlag. At the same instant he could have bitten his tongue for making this thoughtless remark. It must have been caused by studying previous historical representations of the Carthaginian commander in books and images. These representations had so impressed themselves on people's minds, including Silberschlag's, that when hearing or reading the name Hannibal, his figure appeared at once before one's eyes. While studying classical languages at Halle, the history of Rome and Carthage had been taught to him in great detail. Hannibal's achievements had impressed him greatly at the time, though as he became older it seemed to him that the descriptions were very much in favor of the Carthaginians.

Unlike what the Romans were expecting, Hannibal had decided to march via Mont Genèvre. He crossed it with all his 40,000 troops and baggage, with 4000 horses and 37 war elephants.

The exertion must have been unimaginable. It was autumn when the ascent began and November when they reached the summit of the mountains, which were already snow-bound. The paths, little more than boulder-strewn trails, cloudy, fog-shrouded, bordered by abysses, were covered in ice. There was no protection for the animals, no blade of grass. How they endured this is difficult to imagine. That any horses and elephants survived at all borders on the miraculous. As it was, large numbers perished as well as one quarter of the soldiers. Death was a permanent companion on the march. Soldiers and animals succumbed to thirst, to cold, to hunger. They fell by the side and watched the army march on, leaving them behind. Nobody even looked back. It was a tour de force, a masterstroke in staff planning, disposition, reconnaissance, and logistics, which innumerable people paid for with their lives, thus creating for Hannibal an enduring legend, leading to the commander's place in history. Truly, a costly fame.

As Silberschlag looked at the painting, the verses by Matthias Claudius came to his mind and in a low voice he recited:

's ist Krieg! 's ist Krieg! O Gottes Engel wehre,
Und rede du darein!
's ist leider Krieg—und ich begehre
Nicht schuld daran zu sein!

Turner gave him a questioning look. Silberschlag felt suddenly embarrassed and explained that this poem of war was actually about peace. He translated, as well as he could, the first verse:

'It's war. O angel of God, help us, and raise your voice, it's war, and I desire not to be held responsible for it.'

Turner asked him to give a summary of the rest of the verses, with which Silberschlag complied: 'The poet describes how the *I* in the poem would not be able to live with the images of all the dead recurring in his dreams, when the mourning brides, fathers, mothers, wives of the fallen came and mourned in front of him, when plague and hunger ruled and people blamed him that this was all happening because he wanted to earn fame, crown and lands.'

'You see now,' said Turner, 'why you cannot find the general in the painting. *Snow Storm* does not celebrate the power of the individual, such as in an official portrait like *Napoleon at the Saint-Bernard Pass*. My picture expresses man's vulnerability in the face of nature's overwhelming force. Therefore, Hannibal himself is not pictured, and

57

attention is focused upon the victims of the conflict, the struggling soldiers. Yes, it's war, and I don't want to be held responsible for it.

Do you think Napoleon worried about these things when he crossed the Alps and many of his soldiers fell victim to the dreadful strain of the march?'

'Certainly not,' Silberschlag said. 'This villain, as my friend Friedrich called him, was much too greedy for power, and the lives of his soldiers mainly served for his own aggrandizement. But to be fair, I don't want to say that Napoleon did not at the same time believe that he served in some ways the ideals of the French revolution. And at the beginning he did so. And what he achieved in Germany, nolens volens, could have greatly enhanced progress in our country. But alas, it seems that the hopes of our patriots have not been fulfilled. One can only wish that their enraged histrionics will be directed against the real evils. Their great hate for the French was probably more an expression of their inability to change the rule of the princes in their own country into something positive for the people. This may explain what for example our poet Heinrich von Kleist meant in his poem *Germania and her Children,* a poem which in reality is repulsively bloodthirsty. What we find at the end of this distasteful effort is so inhuman that it causes one to shudder: 'Kill the French. You will not be asked for the reasons, come Judgment Day.'

They were silent for a while. Then Turner asked:

'And Goethe, what does he say to such utterings?'

'I have heard Goethe say about Kleist and the other self-styled freedom fighters and advocates for the destruction of the French: 'It is not enough to be well-meaning; one must also foresee the consequences of one's actions.' He dreaded, he said, what these people were attempting because, though it was understandable in the beginning, it was also the beginning of something terrible, which one day would manifest itself in the crassest atrocities. And Goethe was particularly embittered about Kleist's verse 'On Judgment Day you will not be asked for your reasons.' This he found absolutely perfidious because it meant the victors could sanction any deed since they need not be afraid of ever being brought to trial.

I am afraid that my friend Caspar David Friedrich belongs among those who project their despair about the situation in their fatherland onto the French arch-enemy, who is quite convenient for the purpose. There are times when I am inclined to believe that Goethe's words were directly aimed at Friedrich. Though Friedrich expresses his feelings in a quite different, more subtle, I would almost say more honorable way. This shows most clearly in his painting *The Chasseur in the Forest* from 1814. This, Mr. Turner, you should see in order to get a true impression of the art of my friend. Just by explaining it as I am doing now cannot but do it an injustice. But perhaps some day, you will come to Dresden and view Friedrich's paintings and perhaps even meet him in person.'

'This may well be,' answered Turner. 'There is a lot that draws me towards Germany, and you, young friend, awaken a renewed desire in me to get to know the Dresden landscape painters.

As for the German hate of the French I cannot quite follow your reasoning. If I consider what kind of picture we, the English, have of Napoleon and the French revolution, I must say it is no less crass than that of the Germans. And this picture has arisen not against the background of the described hopeless feelings of the subjects of his rule, that is to say it is not based on anything so well founded.

But now listen to what I have written about my painting.'

He stepped nearer to the picture and read from the slip of paper pinned to the frame at the bottom:

'Craft, treachery, and fraud—Salassian force,
Hung on the fainting rear! then Plunder seiz'd
The victor and the captive, Saguntum's spoil,
Alike became their prey; still the chief advanc'd,
Look'd on the sun with hope; —low, broad and wan;
While the fierce archer of the downward year
Stains Italy's blanch'd barrier with storms.
In vain each pass, ensanguin'd deep with dead,
Or rocky fragments, wide destruction roll'd.
Still on Campagnia's fertile plains—he thought,
But the loud breeze sob'd, 'Capua's joys beware!'

Turner became silent, stepped back, and they both continued to look at the painting.

'Your friendly attitude and this image encourage me to speak freely,' Silberschlag said after a while.

'At first sight, or as we would say in German *vordergründig* I recognize in your work the primordial force of the elements to which the smallness of man is subjected, expressed with power and movement, which is increased by the suggestion of the calm boundlessness of the space behind the light. This can present a barrier as well as an opening, a bright future as well as the entrance to hell.'

Turner smiled and remained silent. It was obvious that he liked what his guest told him, and he was waiting for what, after the *vordergründig* would follow.

'But behind that,' Silberschlag continued, 'I can see something which goes much further, something philosophical, if you allow the great word.'

He would have liked to begin this sentence with the word *hintergründig*, in order to continue the German analogy but was unable to find an English equivalent that would express the meaning of *Hintergrund* or background as well as *hintergründig,* which, in meaning, had almost completely lost connection with its main stem.

'So, behind that there seems to me to be an approach to life by the painter, or part of your approach to life, Mr. Turner, which I cannot but call pessimistic.'

His host looked at him in surprise.

'How do you arrive at that, young friend?' he said after a short pause. 'I have never looked at myself that way. And you mean my painting here is so to say a representation of my pessimism?'

'I don't mean it in such a definite way,' answered Silberschlag. 'What I think is that by your way of painting you give the earthly objects in shape and color the character of phenomena which by the almost complete dissolution of perspective ...'

Here Silberschlag paused. He felt he may have gone a bit too far in front of the famous painter. But Turner smiled again and nodded at him encouragingly. So he went on:

'This dissolution of the traditional perspective hardly allows any conclusions as to what is behind the phenomena, namely the objects that cause them. And thus, it is as if in your representation of the world you put in question its perceptibility. And this is what I call philosophic pessimism.'

Turner gave a hearty laugh. 'Oh, you Germans. You never take anything at its face value. There must always be something behind the things, something philosophical, something mysterious, something otherworldly. I wonder if this does not prevent you from acting practically—look at the state your country is in and you see what I mean. Anyway, I need some time to follow such profound philosophical interpretations, such scholarliness.'

To take the sting out of his ironic words, he went to the table, took up the glasses, gave one to Silberschlag and bid him to drink. Then he said:

'If you should be right about what you were saying, then it does not concern me. I paint what my nature orders me to paint without any further thoughts. I only feel that the traditional rules of perspective are no longer sufficient, they don't allow me to express what my soul forces me to bring to light. And so, you have to be satisfied with what you see here before your eyes.'

'What I see before my eyes could not be more satisfying,' Silberschlag said.

'I find your painting overwhelming. But still, the little men, the primordial force of nature, all this gives rise to the impression that human beings are only a temporary phenomenon on this earth and are doomed to disappear sometime. It is as if nature has reached its highest stage of development in the form of man and has at the same time created the means to again get rid of him, having endowed him with the lust to kill, to murder, to wage wars, to suppress and enslave other men, his very brothers.'

Turner was silent for a while. His father came in and replaced some of the tallow candles, which had burnt low. Also, he refilled the glasses and suggested that his son and their guest refresh themselves once more. After doing so, they turned back to the painting.

'The storm, by the way,' Turner said, 'I experienced myself in Yorkshire on a visit with my friend Fawkes in Farnley. This was in November 1811. I remember how I called the son of my friend, Hawkesworth, to come out of the house in order to show him the thunderstorm that was raging over the Wharfe valley. Let me add that at that time there were other, far worse storms, of which you have certainly heard.'

When Silberschlag looked at him questioningly, he went on:

'I mean the storms of the Luddites, and you can take it for a fact that the government sent more troops to Nottinghamshire to suppress the machine breakers and the participants in the bread revolts than Wellington took with him to Spain. There was a mass trial in 1813, some people were hanged, others transported. Do you believe me, Silberschlag, when I say that these political events influence painting and the choice of topics?'

'Absolutely, Mr. Turner. I need only remember some paintings of Friedrich's in which his attitude towards French foreign rule determined his pictorial representation of nature, or rather has been imparted to it. At least one can say that political events have caused the painter to let man and nature interact in a way that the viewer can come to conclusions which are quite separate from the purely aesthetic. But apart from such similarities between English and German landscape painting I see distinct differences between the two.'

His host interrupted him and said, 'Let me make the following proposal. Though in our talk we have come to a topic that interests me most strongly, we should continue it on one of the following days. It is near midnight, and I would not like to let you walk to your inn any later. London might be as modern as it presents itself in broad daylight, but it is still dangerous and eerie at night and most of our streets remain unlighted.

Come here again in two days after breakfast, when it is daylight. And until then, take care.'

Silberschlag was satisfied with the suggestion, because today's impressions were deep and varied, and had to be sorted through and processed so that they could be absorbed and, where required, passed on.

The painter and his father saw him to the door, where he was helped into his coat and handed his hat and umbrella. Then the old man said, 'Now go straight to the 'Old Bell'. Take the lantern, you can bring it back the day after tomorrow.' Silberschlag thanked them again for the fine and instructive evening, and as he made for the inn, he was moved to high spirits by what he had experienced and seen, forgetting about dangers and darkness.

CHAPTER 6

Karl Friedrich Schinkel, Esq.

London, the 24th of November, 1815

Honorable Sir,

I hasten to report to you from London as early as possible and in the greatest detail following the instructions you most graciously conveyed to me at the beginning of this month. These first impressions are not meant to replace the final travel report, both oral and written, that I hope you will be kind enough to graciously receive after my return to Germany.

For reasons of space and time I allow myself for the moment to leave unsaid what should be relayed concerning this enormous city, which on the one hand provides an image of what we too should expect in future regarding municipal development, and on the other hand serves as a warning of what the concentration of an excess of wealth and richness may lead to.

In this letter to you, Sir, I will almost entirely restrict myself to an artist who in my view occupies the most advanced position at the present time among the English landscape painters, particularly in the areas of rural scenery, seascapes, beach scenes as well as vedutas. This painter is Joseph Mallord William Turner, professor of perspective and a member of the Royal Society. After having been allowed to visit him several times in his gallery and after viewing many of his works and comparing them with the paintings of the other masters I am no longer sure if I can still count him among the romanticists. For such a classification his paintings are becoming too expressive and have begun to alter and expand my hitherto existing perception. Two of them I do particularly remember, one from 1813, *Frosty Morning*, and the other from 1812, *Snow Storm. Hannibal and his Army crossing the Alps*. In my eyes both are masterpieces and deserve to be seriously considered for the envisaged selection of paintings.

Frosty Morning is an oil on canvas, ca. 44 by 67 inches. It is a direct but subtle representation of a given moment in time, of a particular day and a season. It records a scene he witnessed and sketched on paper while traveling in Yorkshire. Other people, not the master himself of course, have told me that it includes his eldest daughter, Evelina, and his crop-eared bay horse pulling a cart.

The viewer can clearly see that it is early morning on a sunny winter day. Hedgers and ditchers are starting work in the field, a stage-coach is approaching with its lanterns still lighted. Turner has added a line from Thomson, 'The rigid hoar frost melts before his beams', which describes precisely the phase of the day. Frost has begun to thaw in a few places, so that the ground is brown while in the shadows the frost is still powdered white. The sun, just rising, has not yet managed to dispel the mist. The leafless trees and the foreground weeds are still covered with rime, the long shadows and the silhouetted forms completing Turner's definition of a frosty morning.

The critics for once agreed in praising the work, but no one has purchased it. Therefore, I believe it can still be acquired at an affordable price.

This painting, Sir, shows the painter's impressive power of observation and awakens quite peculiar feelings in the viewer. He wishes to be an inseparable part of the scene and longs at the same time for the warmth and the sanctuary the rising sun promises. The scene is both an immediate experience of the world and a transcendent one, in which the artist goes beyond reality by the emotion his art awakens in the viewer.

While Turner's mythological landscapes, for example the oil on canvas from 1811, *Apollo and Python,* which I also viewed in the master's gallery, seem to avoid this heightened sense of reality were the improbable is simultaneously accepted as the possible, *Frosty Morning* is quite different. It embodies the unity of reality and image; the viewer finds himself in the real world and in the image that the artist creates from it.

Mr. Turner knows about my task here and shows himself willing to discuss the possible sale of some of his paintings. He also accepts that to begin with I can only acquire options on the selected paintings and he realizes that the final decision will be made by you.

Snow Storm, Hannibal and his Army crossing the Alps from 1812 is also oil on canvas and will probably readily meet with the approval of our patriots, since there are distinct parallels to our own most recent past. It could almost be called ironical that shortly after this work was exhibited for the first time the usurper had to retreat ignominiously from Moscow in the terrible Russian winter.

I had a lengthy discussion with Mr. Turner about this painting and it turned out that his opinions about the effects and implications of the picture do not always coincide with mine. But that certainly lies in the nature of art, which is open to subjective approaches.

This painting shows Turner's preference, not to say fascination, with large swirling oval vortexes of wind, rain and cloud, a dynamic composition of contrasting light and dark. The spiral of clouds and the dark winter earth present an enormous void, in which wild, foreboding forces simmer. With this painting the artist gains mastery and dominion over the inner and outer conflict that he has allowed to arise in challenge of our senses.

My words can only inadequately describe the impression that this painting makes on the viewer. Added to all this is the effect of the sun, which despite its pallid light creates a giant gate through which men and animals may either go to hell or to the shimmering plains of Italy.

Honorable Sir, you will not find it easy to avoid similar impressions, when you see the work, even if it seems so far removed from the style of painting common in Germany. By the way, Turner seems to be the only painter in England with whom such wildness, far beyond the norms of traditional perspective, is to be found. I believe that one day you will personally get to know Turner as he has voiced an intention to visit Germany in the foreseeable future. Should that be the case you will find it helpful—as a kind of preparation—to read what Constable, who sat beside Turner at a dinner in the Royal Academy, said about him. Constable had been quite entertained because Turner talked exactly in the way that he had expected: 'He is uncouth, but has a wonderful range of mind.'

He had, it was said, no talent for speaking in public, though I from my experience can say that he in private knew how to put his ideas into words with ease and grace.

I read a transcription of one of Turner's speeches which vividly shows his difficulty in public, namely the stuttering, the long pauses, the bewildering mystery of it. Turner was appealing to artists to stand together for the goods of art and the Royal Academy. This transcription, on a badly printed sheet, circulated among certain people here in London, and I am convinced that the initiators wish the painter ill because they do not understand him and are afraid of his mastership. In truth this speech, which I provide below, shows that he regards the Academy as kind of a family whom he loves and with whom he wishes to stand.

'Gentlemen, I see (pause and another look round) new faces at this—table—Well, do you—do any of you—I mean—Roman history (a pause). There is no doubt, at least I hope not, that you are acquainted—no, unacquainted—that is to say—of course, why not? —you must know something of the old—ancient—Romans. (Loud applause). Well, sirs, those old people—the Romans I allude to—were a warlike set of people—yes, they were—because they came over here, you know, and had to do a great deal of fighting before they arrived, and after too. Ah! that they did, and they always fought in a phalanx—know what that is? (Hear, hear, said some one.) Do you know sir? Well, if you don't, I will tell you. They stood shoulder to shoulder, and won everything. (Great cheering). Now, then, I have done with the Romans, and I come to the old man and the bundle of sticks—Aesop, ain't he? — fables, you know—all right—yes, to be sure.'

There are, Sir, many outstanding painters in England, among whom I would like to set apart John Constable with his pleasant representation of the English landscape, and George Morland, whose hallmark is humble life in the country and whose work *Outside the Ale House* from 1792 I remember for its excellent and reassuring vision of rural timelessness.

Nor are the names of Reynolds and Gainsborough, who are no longer among the living, unknown in Germany.

Now a few words about Turner's way of painting, which I would designate as open. It is the technique that uses color beginnings as an element of chance, as a mere accident, in the act of painting. This is one of the reasons that he does not like being watched while working since chance is not something he can anticipate. People here like to cite an anecdote—and I do not think they are always well-meaning—which goes as follows. In order to create blots on the canvass, from which he can start creating further details and finally the whole picture—he allows little children to slap with their hands on the painting to create the aforementioned blots. Another anecdote maintains that the drawing of a man-of-war began with a crumpled and color-stained paper ball.

In this connection I would like to come back to John Constable. To me it is a remarkable example of the individualism in English painting that two contemporaries such as Constable and Turner can be so different in their art— while the differences between our German, our Dresden landscapers are not always recognizable, apart, of course, from Friedrich.

Criticism or an aesthetic evaluation of these two extraordinary painters—even a comparison—should not be attempted. Still, the range of Turner's world of ideas and his depth of thought are to be placed above Constable's. And his truly new approach to art which goes beyond tradition that challenges the rules of perspective, that creates a virtual explosion of light and color and presents a completely different view of the phenomena of the world that reaches far into the future, all these find their incredible expression only through this artist.

Hoping, Honorable Sir, that this report, which will be followed by others, serves His Majesty the King's and your plans for the new museum, I submissively remain your humble servant Silberschlag.

Postscript: I am making use of the permission that you, Sir, gave me in Berlin and will send a copy of this letter to Excellency Goethe in Weimar.

PART 2
MEISSEN, MAY 1816

CHAPTER 7

Not far before Meissen, on the right bank of the Elbe river below Sörnewitz a wanderer came to rest on a tree trunk that had washed ashore.

With long strides he had traveled the last two miles on the old towpath and had advanced so well that he could now enjoy an hour of repose before sunrise, a time that was sacred to him.

The appearance of this man with his gaunt, angular body, his ash blond hair and beard, his blue eyes and expressive face resembled the image Germans had of their Germanic fathers, particularly in times of patriotic fervor. His sturdy gnarled stick and the beard he wore that covered his neck but exposed his chin served to enhance this impression.

His face was characterized by a look of melancholy. His eyes, set deep in their sockets, seemed to gaze at the world in a manner both curious and guarded, in an effort to determine the reality of the environment around him and the significance hidden behind it.

To the north-west, in the dawn, he could already discern though dimly the houses and towers of the city of Meissen. His eyes searched for the pyramidal-shaped steeple of the cathedral which was the destination of his present wandering.

It was cold, the night had been clear, the last twinkling of the stars was still to be seen. White early morning mist hung over the water so that the wanderer could only indistinctly see the southern bank with its alders and willows where a fisherman sat in his boat not far from the bank. The wanderer wore a peak cap made of linen, which he now took off in order to wipe the sweat from his forehead. He leaned on his stick, which had served to carry his knapsack, having been pushed through the handle and thrown over his shoulder.

In order to breathe more freely, he opened his long jacket and the high collar of his shirt.

His long trousers, rather tight on his legs, reached down to his shoes.

Opening his knapsack, he took out a heel of bread, a piece of cheese, dried plums and a bottle of water. He put everything on the tree trunk beside him, took a knife from his jacket pocket and opened it. Then he pulled the plug from the bottle and drank.

The evening of the last day had been spent in the Grand Enclosure, a large deer park, which lay to the northwest, outside the gates of Dresden on the south bank of the Elbe river. There he had observed the sunset and the dusk, which were his beloved times.

A parkway lined with trees is seen by the observer as the path of life, which from a narrow and shadowed space leads to the freedom of a heavenly existence. To the wanderer, the river seems to be a modification of this idea. In the foreground it shows itself as a shallow stretch of water, divided into several rivulets. This will without doubt cause the sailboat to run aground, a symbol of death, though for the wanderer it is glorified by the play of the colors of the sky reflected by the water.

The observer sees the pale blue of the sky in harmony with the brown-violet of the swampy ground. When the time comes, this harmony will be for him the promise of a heavenly existence, a consolation in his hour of dying. One day the movement of the ship will be a symbol of his own fate; it runs aground, but a bridge of promise, faith and hope will help the uneasy wanderer to reach the other, the heavenly bank. The sun has set, no ray falls on the earth, and the only light is provided by the reflection from the sky. This, however, is full of bright colors and the consolation dispensed by Christ during the impending night, in the hour of fear and pain of death.

The observer will store the scene in his memory, and some day the painter will paint it in oil as a symbol of a Christian death.

When the dusk had deepened and the reflection of the sun in the sky had disappeared, the wanderer—the painter Caspar David Friedrich—paid a fisherman a small fare to take him over the river to Kötitz, where he spent the rest of the night in a wayside inn.

Years ago, the village had been completely destroyed in a fire, but rebuilt. It was now prospering through its proximity to the great river, which, though always a threat, was also a source of life, as proven by the quality of the food and the accommodations to be had at the inn.

From there the painter had started on the towpath toward Meissen and then, almost within sight of it, rested before starting on the last section of the way.

Dining on what he had left in his knapsack, he looked over the river towards the town and pondered. His frugal breakfast, his not quite clean neckerchief, his sense of having no real home, now, in his forty-second year, made him reflect on the conditions of his life.

His domicile was in a house by the river in Pirna, a suburb of Dresden, a neighborhood of residents who had small income and limited assets. The furniture in his room mirrored his status, consisting of a wooden chair and a table, on which the tools of his occupation were seen. If he had a visitor, another old wooden chair had to be fetched, if he had two visitors, a wooden bench from the porch by the stairs was carried in. In the chamber adjacent to the room there was only a table, old as the chair, and an ancient bed with a woolen blanket.

Friedrich felt he did not need the comforts of middle-class, had even talked himself into believing such comfort would keep him from concentrating on his work, the preconditions of which, he was convinced, were the intensity and solitude of the artist's way of life.

But lately he had become less certain. Looking around he observed that almost all men, whom he valued, had taken wives. His young friend Silberschlag had found himself a wife and had related what this experience was like, which was amusing, if nothing else. A man then has a household, however small. The wife comes into the study to tell her husband to come and have lunch. And it is likewise amusing that one stays home at night, in the warm nest, instead of walking around in God's free nature. Whatever one does, from then on, is always done with regard to the wife. Even a nail has to be hammered into the wall so that the wife can reach up to what hangs from it. One eats more, drinks more, hugs and kisses, and spends more money.

Suddenly the old furniture is no longer good enough. New things are bought and one hardly recognizes one's own house. On the other hand, everything looks cleaner and nicer, as if by magic.

Also, things are suddenly needed which one never dreamed of before: Coffee tin, coffee grinder, coffee bag, coffee pot, coffee funnel, crucibles and jars, everything is urgently needed, even spittoons are placed everywhere so that one can no longer use the whole room.

More kisses and hugs, Silberschlag had said. How does one go about that, hugging and kissing? And how does one endure the woman changing everything? If he, Friedrich, was ever placed in a situation like that, in his own place, which was living room and studio combined, everything would have to remain as it always was.

To take a wife, how is that accomplished? And even if one succeeded, what then? What is one supposed to do with her, always presuming one had the means to support her and oneself and the expected children and still uphold the standards befitting one's social status?

Friedrich knew a woman from his neighborhood, almost twenty years younger than he, the daughter of the manager of a dye trading establishment, thus a respectable middle-class daughter, whom he thought suitable if a life partner was at all necessary.

Christiane Caroline Bommer was a humble and quiet woman, and she had a fifteen-year-old brother, Christoph Wilhelm, who at that early age showed great interest in painting, in which Friedrich encouraged him.

A previous attempt on Friedrich's part to find a suitable bride had failed, causing great embarrassment and much blushing. The painter had often observed the sister of the stationer, from whom he used to buy his pencils, sitting and working behind the window of the shop.

It seems to him that she is nice, sweet-natured and modest. He thinks that if this friendly girl would live in his home, then in the evenings when coming home or after ending his painting for the day, he would certainly not miss the absence of passionate affection, which he now, despite the trembling of her bodice when speaking, feels is still lacking. He exchanges a few not very significant words with her, and even these he only manages to stutter with a tightened throat. But still he resolves, on the spot, to bravely buy a few pencils (which he does not really need) early the next day and use this occasion to question the pretty maiden to discover whether it might lead to a more intimate conversation with her. He makes his way to the shop with his heart beating wildly, because women, there can be no doubt, are strange, mysterious and difficult beings and fill one with all sorts of fears. Also, their physicality was something the painter had knowledge of only from a certain, safe distance having tried his hand at nude painting. What is it that hides there and fills a man with anxiety, what is it that burdens one's dreams with anxieties and sometimes leads to a soiling desire?

In short, the artist, tired of his lonely home, referred to as his hermitage by some, having prepared himself mentally, succeeds in arranging a meeting on the same evening in the shop with his adored.

The evening makes him a happy bridegroom, and with joyous heart he feels he must tell everybody, must spread the news everywhere. Then comes the first disturbance to his exulted state. A friend wants to know the name of the bride, and alas! the painter, who has been a bit premature in calling himself a bridegroom, realizes he has forgotten, or he even forgot to ask for it.

No wonder that now a state of disillusionment sets in, strengthened the next day by the question, what does one do in the bedchamber with such a creature, assuming the relation turns out well and ends in marriage?

That he had not found out the name of his bride causes a general delight among his friends and acquaintances and confirms the unworldliness and shyness of their friend, which they had often bewailed.

As Friedrich felt the first rays of the sun rising behind him in the east, he continued to think about women. He must try to be more successful with the maiden Bommer than he was with his first courtship.

But how should he answer the big question of what to do with a woman in the decisive moments? Perhaps he could ask the doctor of medicine Karl Gustav Carus, who had for two years been practicing as Director of the Maternity Clinic in Dresden the somewhat weird profession of Professor of the Art of Delivery. Carus was also a painter, and a friend had recently mentioned to Friedrich at an exhibition that the doctor had expressed views on landscape painting which he found very interesting. But until then Friedrich had not had a chance to meet the doctor, and so far had shied away from approaching him with the explicit request for enlightenment, though he thought that someone whose profession was to assist with the results of physical love must have a thorough knowledge of the female anatomy and would certainly know about the procedure which brought about those results.

He took a booklet from his knapsack, which the bookseller Helmert, also known as Diogenes, had, with the wink of an eye, sold to him after wrapping it carefully in brown paper.

This shabby bookseller, often picked on and mocked, pursued his antiquarian business on the New Market, at and on the big water trough, which stood in front of the Salomonis apothecary.

A Guide before, during and after Cohabitation or a comprehensible Instruction to practice Cohabitation in such a way that Health will not be impaired, and the Propagation of the Human Race by beautiful, healthy and strong Children will be promoted.

The author was one Dr Becker, and the sixth edition of the book had been published in Leipzig at the beginning of the year.

Friedrich read in the Preface: 'Among all the subjects which attract the attention of the youth as well as the old man there seems to be none as important and as appealing as the one treated in this writ. It was my desire to help spread more light among the better classes. To bring up some of the things

81

that everybody should know about but which only few have knowledge of. Several people have voiced the wish, particularly the venerable Privy Councilor Hufeland in his Macrobiotics, that a booklet for the newly married be written and published which would teach them the (physical) purpose of the wedlock, the means to achieve this purpose without compromising the other aims of marriage. The author would be glad if impartial judges said that he has achieved this aim.'

So Hufeland, whom Excellency Goethe estimated so highly, was called upon as a guide. But if the book was about only the physical side, how would that be of assistance? One could probably master that, but the most important aspect was never mentioned, namely how shame and shyness caused by exposure, how feelings of powerlessness in front of the female body and the mind-boggling surrender of one's own individuality could be transformed into something beneficial for a family and one's artistic work.

Other things, like his financial situation, were no longer a great obstacle to marriage. For about 6 years, since anno '10, his living conditions had much improved. His oil paintings *The Abbey in the Oakwood* and *The Monk by the Sea* had been sold to the Prussian King. Urged on by his son, the fifteen-year-old crown prince, and despite limited means caused by political circumstances, the King had paid 450 thalers for them at the Berlin Academy exhibition of 1810. The Prince was known for his youthful enthusiasm for everything romantic and Gothic, which thank God was kept within the boundaries of good taste by his art adviser, the painter and architect Schinkel. In 1812, the King purchased another painting, exhibited in Weimar, *Morning in the Giant Mountains,* for a similar sum.

In addition, the artist had been appointed Foreign Member of the Berlin Academy, and he had hopes of being accepted by the Dresden Arts Academy, which promised an annuity of 150 thalers, not a great amount, but certainly helpful.

These honors as well as the controversy arising over his painting *Cross in the Mountains,* which he had exhibited in his house anno 08, and his inclusion in Meusel's *Teutsches Künstlerlexicon* had helped to make his name known and raised the public's interest in his works so that their sale was at least moderately promoted. The patriotic enthusiasm in the times of the war against Napoleon also contributed to his reputation.

While the painter pondered these things, the sun had risen higher, and Meissen now presented itself more clearly in the morning light. The mist above the river had dissolved. The contours of the landscape, shaped by human activity, emerged quite distinctly, and Friedrich felt capable of coming to a decision with regard to the maiden Bommer. Perhaps the women themselves were able and willing to help the inexperienced and awkward male into the position required for the foundation of a family.

Friedrich finished his bread and water and in a good mood started on the final part of his journey to the Meissen cathedral.

CHAPTER 8

Meissen Cathedral is a subject of great interest and admiration. People praise it as a masterpiece of pure Gothic architecture, with a tower of graceful trellis work 78 meters high. When it was destroyed by lightning in 1547, some say it was God's punishment for the belated conversion of the city's Christians to the new Lutheran faith.

This was not the first time it was destroyed. The building founded by the marvelous emperor Otto I had been laid waste by fire at the beginning of the 13th century. The construction of the present cathedral lasted almost two hundred years and was finished in the middle of the fifteenth century. It is to be regretted that the purely Gothic impression is impaired by the addition of the burial chapel ordered by Prince Elector Frederick the Belligerent. He had it built as a resting place for his dynasty. Now it obscures the beautiful main portal with its rich collection of figures. On the other hand, the fine figures and colors of the portal had been preserved, and are now enclosed and protected from the rigors of the weather.

A second addition was the burial chapel of Duke George the Bearded and his spouse Barbara. Right off the South Portal is the Chapel of John, an excellent example of the noble spirit of early Gothic architecture and an object of constant admiration by Friedrich. The sculptures, here and in the chancel, of Emperor Otto and his spouse Adelheid, of St. Donatus, of the two Johns and Virgin Mary are from the same time. There are also old stained-glass paintings and a winged altar painting in the chancel which depict the adoration of the Magi.

Friedrich entered the cathedral from the cloister through a door that the sexton, a friend of his, had unlocked for him. It was cold, still and dusky. The air smelled musty and damp. Friedrich pulled the neckerchief from his jacket pocket and laid it around his neck against the chill. He had taken it off while climbing the path from the Elbe through the hollow way and over the steps to the castle bridge in the warm morning sun. Inside the cathedral, he buttoned up his jacket. Then with slow steps he walked to the right through the rood screen and approached the altar. The sun was already shining through the windows. Its rays spread through the chancel and created colored reflections on the stone floor before his feet.

His eyes follow the sun beams up to the origin of their color, the middle window, a fine example of Gothic stained-glass painting from the middle of the 13th century. Represented are the kings of the old testament, led by Christ as the ruler of the world. Scenes from the life of Christ, from his passion, crucifixion, resurrection as well as sacrificial scenes from the Old Testament are to be admired. For quite a while Friedrich cannot detach himself from the image of Christ, his savior.

Then Goethe comes to his mind, who, when visiting him in his studio in Dresden, had particularly praised the purity of the cathedral's high Gothic architecture with the following words, which he can still remember:

'This cathedral is the slenderest and most beautiful building of that time that I know of, not darkened by any monuments, not impaired by galleries, but painted in yellow, lighted by white glass windows and only colored by the central window of the chancel.'

And he had urgently advised Friedrich to visit the cathedral, a piece of advice that the painter had followed several times, as he had written His Excellency.

He steps aside as he shies from treading on the colored reflections, which seem to him a promise of hope in the darkened, seemingly endless tranquility of the vast building.

As always when visiting the cathedral Friedrich first directs his steps toward an old tabernacle in the chancel which hardly differs from a little wall cabinet for storing bread and cheese, yet hides a nightmarish and menacing secret. If you approach it and put your ear near it, as Friedrich is doing now, you hear a weird roaring, rushing and moaning which seem to come from a fire burning in a bottomless abyss. In catholic times, so the narrative goes, the Canonici of the Cathedral chapter, behind the back of the bishop and without his knowledge, told the congregation, who lived in permanent fear of hell, that this was a bricked-up access to purgatory. If necessary, it could be opened to send earthly sinners down to the fire where they would be properly fried and purified and set on the path of righteousness. After sufficient time, let's say a few centuries, sometimes a few thousand years depending on the number and gravity of their sins, they could be hauled back to earth and in the end find a peaceful and blessed end. The faithful could, and of course they regularly and understandably did, spare themselves this fiery purification by a generous donation to the canons. When the bishop learned about this aberration from the rightful Catholic teaching, which as everyone should know, taught that death had to come before purgatory and that afterwards one went directly to heaven and not back to earth, the bishop rained on them a holy thunderstorm and forced them to end this heresy. Naturally they soon found other means to fleece their sheep and thus increase their already substantial income.

Friedrich abhorred this popish nonsense, but was still intrigued by the story and the place. The thought of death, which occurred to him at this moment, was familiar and offered a certain consolation. The chance of withdrawing of one's own accord from this earthly vale of tears, from the guilt with which one inevitably loaded onto oneself just by living, was very calming. He imagined paradise as an eternal, dreamless sleep, an escape from the lack of understanding among the critics and the public, from the effort of unerringly following one's own way as well as the deep disappointment about the political situation. The idea of a conscious and timely departure from earth was very alluring, supposing that God would forgive this deadly sin, despite what the church was teaching.

He hoped that God had forgiven a deed he had attempted many years ago. During a period of utter desperation as a young man he had sought to end his life by directing a knife at his own neck. Afterward there remained a sense of guilt as well as the desire to hide the sign of what he had attempted by cultivating sideburns, which covered the scar on his neck.

He thought of his childhood and the fragmentary memories he had of goodness and warmth, but also of indelible recollections of guilt and failure. He looked back to a land he had left and would never again return to. His life, it seemed to him, was filled with pleasure, fear and guilt, accompanied by certain colors, contours, smells and sounds forming a string of indelible memories, which he clung to as if he could win from them insights into the future. His encounter with death seemed to explain to him in a dark and symbolic way why he had become a painter, a creator of his kind of paintings.

The painter walks back to the rood screen, followed by the stern look of St Donatus, who stands above him on a stone pedestal under a canopy to the left of the door to the treasure chamber. He turns around once again and casts a glance on the stony figures of Emperor Otto and his consort Adelheid, the founders of the bishopric of Meissen. Clearly, the Naumburg master sculptor had succeeded in their attitude, their gesture and their expression in creating a relationship between them.

What a singular ruler Otto had been, who saw as his vocation the improvement of the reputation of the German nation and the internal and external strengthening of the empire. In that he differed from many of today's potentates, except perhaps for the Prussian King Frederick William III. Otto's first wife, granddaughter of Alfred the Great, the Anglo-Saxon princess Editha, whom he had loved tenderly, had died when he was thirty-four years old. Five years later he married the widow of Lothair, King of Italy, Adelheid, who had asked for his help against Berengar, Margrave of Ivrear. From then on, he called himself King of Italy. Now they stand there hewn in stone, turned toward each other for all eternity, in the High Choir.

Friedrich walks through the central nave to the princes' chapel and from there through the door to the funeral chapel, which was added to the south side of the burial chamber by the last catholic duke of the Albertine line, George.

Friedrich now stands before the altar triptych of Cranach the Elder from 1534. It shows Christ's stigmata, a favorite motif of both the master and his time. The Man of Sorrows is mourned by Mary and John. A swarm of angels bring the instruments of Christ's sufferings. The left image shows Duke George with the apostles Jacob the Elder and Peter, on the right one can see Duchess Barbara with the apostles Paul and Andrew.

Friedrich stands lost in thought looking at the Christ who died for his sins. He admires the artistry of the painter and recognizes the naivety in the execution of the picture which has roots in a period when altar images were used to tell the people about biblical events. How wonderful the master's clear colors are preserved. Certainly, Lucas Cranach was a Christian in a quite simple and uncomplicated sense and hardly affected by any religious doubts. Friedrich wishes he, too, could be thus. Life and art would certainly be less complicated, though then his painting would resemble the usual depiction of the Christian story and the common presentation of the well beaten path, where every ass carries its sack, where dog and cat perambulate because it's safe, because the famous artists of antiquity were held up as models and examples for a thousand years. No, times have changed. Cranach, you venerable and simple man, I must be different and my altar must look different from yours and the altars of your followers.

Against the opposite wall he finds a stool, on which to sit and, leaning his head against the wall, he closes his eyes.

'O yes, Sir, Chamberlain von Ramdohr, widely traveled art critic and diplomat,' he thinks, 'with the *Cross in the Mountains* I painted my very own religious landscape, the landscape of my faith, in which God is part of nature and at the same time beyond nature and the netherworld, because he is the universe itself.'

Suddenly he hears a voice speaking to him from the direction of the altar painting:

'Mr. Friedrich, what a strange religiosity, yours and that of your sponsors. How fast after the marriage has the ducal couple, Theresa Anna Maria and Franz Anton von Thun-Hohenstein hung your work in their bedroom, your painting that was allegedly intended for their Tetschen castle chapel. Has it ever hung in the chapel at all? They had probably submitted to the mysticism which sneaks into everything nowadays and which wafts at us from the arts as well as from science, from philosophy as well as from religion like a narcotic haze. Obviously the newly married have regarded the union of God and landscape as an invitation to take part in God's act of creation.'

'Sir Chamberlain von Ramdohr, God is the universe, and the mystery of the direct encounter with God is the unconditional belief in the incarnation of his son, who shines here in the purple of the sunset, not by himself, but illuminated by God the Father. This cannot be misunderstood or falsely interpreted. And what you said about the place where the picture was hung, is ridiculous. As if this place could harm the painting. No, Ramdohr, please be good enough to come out of your past. You want me to paint history as it has been painted for centuries, as did Cranach over there, without any reference to God as an inherent part and at the same time master of nature.'

Friedrich hears the voice of his and his friends' adversary loud and clear:

'I am certain, Mr. Friedrich, you and the likes of you don't know what you are doing. You don't paint the Christian message but your subjective interpretation of it, the picture of it that you carry inside yourself. If one believes you, then Christian teaching is presenting individual emotion, declining any dogma, forgetting that dogma or doctrine is one of the preconditions of true faith. With this you disturb the faithful and cast them into doubt because you take away the main supports of their belief. You should know better. Those who throw God's children into doubt fall into sin.'

Friedrich starts from his half-slumber and looks around. He looks at the triptych. What a strange but yet distinct dream. O Chamberlain Friedrich Wilhelm Basilius von Ramdohr, art enthusiast and author of art books, you are constantly in my mind because you incarnate all who look at my works with the eyes of the past centuries.

The painter stood up, left chapel and tomb and walked slowly back through the nave. The sun had risen towards midday so that he saw the colored reflections of the choir window only on the steps to the altar.

The walls and mighty pillars, built for eternity, awakened in him the desire to become one with them, part of their nature, which is of divine origin, and by taking part in their eternal permanence to be nearer to God. His landscapes and paintings of ruins were also part of this yearning. Ramdohr and his likes could of course never understand this.

Suddenly he hears that the door of the west portal is opened. He turns around and sees the pastor of St Afra hurrying towards him. It is good that this friend, who is dear to his heart, comes to tear him out of his fruitless brooding.

CHAPTER 9

The pastor was a well-nourished man, whose rosy face could not express the severity he felt his position sometimes required. The sinful sheep of his parish liked attending his services, because he did not preach about the grim, murderous, irascible, permanently offended and punishing God of the Old Testament, who, if people did not obey him like slaves, killed, destroyed and struck them with boils, persecuted them with the plague, even visiting punishment on children and cattle, and anything they possessed.

No, Reverend Gottlieb was a cheerful Christian, for whom the Lord was the God of love, of forgiveness and not of hell. To him, hell, like the alleged purgatory behind the tabernacle in the chancel of the cathedral, were inventions of the old church (which regrettably continued with some of the same practices in the new one, too) used to keep people in fear and obedience. Of course, he was prudent enough to keep these views to himself. The Church council was strict and had already rebuked him several times for what they called the lax execution of his office. But since highly respected and influential members of his flock supported him, he had so far been able to avoid being sent to another, less prominent parish.

He wore a high-necked frock coat with a single row of buttons, under which his stomach bulged. The small stand-up collar was freshly starched, and his head was uncovered.

Reverend Gottlieb, despite his jolly manner, was a serious man, who had seen worse times and not forgotten them. During the Battle of Nations AD 1813 he had been an army chaplain with the Saxon army corps and had, with a part of the Saxon troops, deserted and gone over to the Allies on the 18th of October. Some of the deserters were among the 6,000 who had survived Napoleon's retreat from Moscow, which was all that remained of the original 21,000. The agonies of the soldiers suffered during the retreat cannot be put into words, and those who had been quickly killed by the Cossacks and Russian peasants could regard themselves as lucky.

After the Battle of Leipzig thousands of the wounded and the dying, among them a considerable number of French, were carried into the churches in Leipzig, which had been transformed into military hospitals. There they fell into the hands of the surgeons who sawed, hacked, cut and cauterized the wounds while men moaned and screamed. The scene could break one's heart. Moreover, the hospital fever raged so that only few succeeded in coming out alive. Daily the dead, robbed of their clothes, were thrown out of the windows onto the streets, and large rack wagons were filled to the brim with dead. The wagoners stepped on the dead bodies while stacking them and worked with rolled up sleeves as if they were handling wooden logs. Often, soldiers refused to be taken to the hospitals because they believed they would certainly die there. They preferred crouching on a street corner or on the stairs of a house in the dim hope of survival.

Reverend Gottlieb tried to dispense consolation wherever he could, and jotted down the last words of many in order to take them, and if this was not possible at least send them to their mothers, fathers, sisters, brides and wives left behind.

The horrors he witnessed did not embitter him towards the people who caused such great suffering to one another. Rather, it only increased his sense of pity.

Unlike his friend Caspar David Friedrich, he could not, despite what he had experienced, share the hate his fellow countrymen felt for the French. He had seen too many of them dying or dead, and he would never forget the images of the retreat of the French from Leipzig. The regiments broken up and in dissolution stumbled through the streets and mixed with baggage carts, cattle, ammunition wagons and guns. Left lying were overturned carts, dead and wounded soldiers, horses whose bowels hung out of their bodies and had become tangled in their legs as they desperately tried to get up. And all this happened under the continuous thunder of guns and the flashes of powder.

He patiently endured the reproaches leveled at him for aiding the Catholic enemies with the same Christian charity that he granted the Saxons. He could have pointed to the doctor and painter Carus—though he did not—who disregarding all national barriers had in 1813 become head physician of a French military hospital, for which he had even been promised the order of the Legion of Honor.

It was not without reason that of all of Friedrich's paintings the pastor liked best *The Chasseur in the Forest*.

With this painting of a soldier lost in a wood, Friedrich portrays his inevitable fate, symbolized by the dark forest in front of him and the bird of death behind him. Wherever the soldier goes, backward or forward, death awaits him. The depiction is however without hate, rather with a sort of mourning compassion. The painter had allowed the pastor to have the painting, remarking that he could keep it until a buyer was found. Interested persons would be sent to Gottlieb where they could view the work.

Beside *The Tomb of Arminius* this painting had been one of the main attractions of the Patriotic Art Exhibition initiated by the Russian Governor General Prince Repnin in March 1814 to celebrate the liberation of Dresden.

During the military events Friedrich had withdrawn for more than eight months to the quiet and graceful village of Krippen on the Elbe opposite Schandau in Saxon Switzerland because he thought he was unsuited for military service. But he bravely supported his friend Kersting, who wanted to join Lützow's Free Corps and needed to purchase equipment. Friedrich's support for the war did not end here; under the impact of Theodor Körner's heroic death he wrote a fervently patriotic poem, in which he celebrated and mourned the fallen warriors of the fight against Napoleon.

Gottlieb had gotten to know Friedrich when he, himself an art enthusiast and follower of the new landscape painting, regularly saw the painter in his studio in Dresden and knew almost all of his works. He grew to like the gruff and sometimes gloomy and melancholy man and set himself the task, whenever possible, of cheering him up and making him acquainted with the friendly side of the Christian faith. And Friedrich was grateful for this, because he was aware of his own mental state, a certain heightened sensitivity under which he suffered. Of course, he would have liked to escape from it, at least every now and then, but at the same time he believed that this frame of mind was the precondition for following his very own path as an artist.

It was not to be wondered that Reverend Gottlieb had supported the painter in his dispute with Basilius von Ramdohr. He had even done so, though in a somewhat disguised manner, in his sermons by speaking against people who despised their neighbors simply because they held different opinions. Quite openly, though, he had, under the pseudonym Deo Gratias, published commentaries in the *Journal des Luxus und der Moden* that supported Friedrich's new approach.

'My dear Friedrich,' he called out, when there were still fifteen paces between them. 'How good of you to see us in Meissen today. The sexton has lost no time telling me about your visit here in the cathedral.' He hurried toward the painter with outstretched hands, which Friedrich grasped and shook with a good-natured smile.

'Reverend Gottlieb, good to see you after the visitations by Ramdohr.'

'You must be joking, Ramdohr here?' He looked searchingly around.

'No, not in the flesh, but he visited me in spirit while I was sitting and dreaming, there in the chapel, in front of Cranach's painting. The old stories come up again and again and make me grieve, not so much because of their criticism, but because of their cold lack of understanding. Only heartless and stupid art judges, whose writings have damaged many a tender soul, can believe that there is just one way to create art, namely their own.'

'Yes, dear friend, you are certainly right. Only, can we expect otherwise? Is not a cold realism coming to the surface, now, as the patriotic fervor has almost dissipated and all the promises made to the nation are broken, a realism whose protagonists want to remove everything secretive and instinctual from art? Only think what Excellency Goethe nowadays voices about our landscapers, and even our admired Schinkel in Berlin seems to have forgotten how he himself only recently painted. Though, to be fair, he devotes himself these days almost entirely to architecture, and we can be sure that he will achieve much more in this field than he did in painting.'

With these words Gottlieb turned toward the exit, took the painter by the arm and drew him along.

'Come, friend, it will soon be midday and my wife has prepared a meal that will certainly suffice for a guest, who is unexpected but all the more welcome.'

Leaving the cathedral, they passed the Kornhaus, went through the Domplatz, then over the Schlossbrücke, and turned left into the Schlossgasse. Going down the Red Steps, they passed St. Afra to their right and soon reached the vicarage Freiheit No. 7.

The name *Freiheit* derived from the independence the local residents enjoyed from the rest of the city. They were not subjected to the city's jurisdiction and were free from any duties, though not allowed to practice a trade associated with the guilds. That meant that here resided ecclesiastical chapters with their courts and landed gentry who lived on their large estates ringed by high walls. The church of St. Afra was the dominant feature. Together with the adjacent cloister courtyard it belonged to the former Augustinian monastery.

All of this was lovingly recounted by Reverend Gottlieb, though he knew that Friedrich was familiar with the history of Meissen. Gottlieb loved Meissen and allowed no chance to pass without expressing this.

The friends stopped in front of the vicarage which, with its buttresses and small windows not much bigger than loopholes attested to its great age. The bay windows from the renaissance depicted Peter and Paul, and the house had probably been a former fortified tower. Such fortress homes, erected before the town had been walled in, could be found in many other places on the *Freiheit* and in Meissen. Of all this Gottlieb did not hesitate to inform his guest before they entered.

Frau Gottlieb, who had frequently received Friedrich in her home, welcomed him warmly. She was a small, delicate woman, who wore a long dark dress with a high waistline and a collar that hid her neck. Her hair was covered with a hood, which was bound under her chin. She had hastily removed her white apron on seeing her husband approaching with a visitor. The sleeves of her dress were adorned with frills and wristbands. On her right hand she wore an iron ring, having sacrificed her golden wedding ring following an appeal of the Spener'sche Zeitung in Berlin. The newspaper had called on the people in Germany to help financing the struggle against Napoleonic foreign rule by contributing their wedding rings and other jewels. In exchange they received rings of iron inscribed 'Gold I gave for Iron'. As Saxony was allied with Napoleon, this had to be done secretly in Dresden, and a friend had taken the ring and jewels to Berlin, where they were presented to the authorities. It was not until the final defeat of the French that she could show her iron ring openly.

Her husband and his friend went to the dining hall where the table was already laid. The Gottliebs liked substantial meals, not only on Sundays, and Frau Gottlieb always saw to it that they had a competent maid to assist in the kitchen, since she liked to do the cooking herself.

When they were on the point of taking their seats at the table the children entered boisterously, the five-year-old twins Charlotte and Luise and four-year-old Karl. They clamored jubilantly around the guest, who with a smile bent down and stroked their heads.

Friedrich loved children, which they sensed, and therefore they loved the odd tall man in return, sometimes exploiting his good nature, which he patiently tolerated, playing with them whenever possible or drawing for them whatever they demanded.

In Dresden a little girl from his neighborhood constantly begged for little drawings on paper and took them home carefully. The painter was pleased with the interest of the child and one day asked her what she did with all those drawings. She answered, somewhat astounded by the stupidity of the master: 'But I need them for wrapping up my bread and dripping that mummy gives me when I stroll with my friends.'

After they had all settled down around the table, the maid served the meal.

First came a plate with a large breaded brisket of beef, finely garnished with cooked vegetables from the vicarage garden. A small bowl with boiled potatoes and a basket with thick slices of dark rye bread stood ready on the table. The potatoes were the last from last year's crop and had kept well in the dry and airy cellar. The Saxons had not long before become familiar with this new supplement, and its popularity was quickly growing.

Ilse, the maid, coming from Silesia, had become acquainted with this earth fruit in her homeland, where, as in Pomerania, Old Fritz, Frederick II of Prussia, had by force introduced the potato. Potato farming on a large scale only began at the end of the past century. Before that potatoes were grown in gardens, though on heavy and wet soil the crops were small. Ilse was the one who cared for the potatoes, hoeing, mounding, watering and finally storing the potato crop in the cellar.

After saying grace, the host took the big carving knife and cut the joint into thick even slices, which he put on the plates that the family and their guest held out to him.

Frau Gottlieb had started the preparation of the meal early in the kitchen. Ilse had bought the large brisket the day before at the local butcher's and cooked it for three hours in beef bouillon. This was accomplished on an open hearth and took time since they had to feed the fire constantly with wood.

After that, Frau Gottlieb placed the cooked meat in a skillet with a few spoonfuls of fat skimmed from the bouillon. Then the meat was covered with breadcrumbs mixed with fat. It was salted and put into the oven preheated by the open-hearth fire. There the joint remained until it had assumed a fine light brown color.

In the meantime, Ilse used the now free hearth for cooking the vegetables, carrots and white turnips, in beef bouillon. The cores of two cabbage heads, cut into thick wedges and cooked in fatty bouillon and ground nutmeg, which normally belonged to this dish, could not be served, the time of the year not allowing.

The small lunch party eagerly devoted themselves to the meal, and Friedrich, in whose bachelor household in Dresden the meals were never so rich, ate heartily. The two twin sisters had very good table manners while of course Karl needed the attention of Frau Gottlieb, who cut his bites for him and encouraged him to use his little spoon to shove the food into his mouth. The maid took her meal in the kitchen beside the sink.

The table talk, which was mainly furnished by Pastor Gottlieb and the painter, while Frau Gottlieb was busy with the children, concerned itself with the economic consequences of the war and division of Saxony as well as the attitude of the King, Frederick Augustus. Gottlieb thought it extraordinarily characteristic that the King, having returned from Prussian captivity one day after the withdrawal of the Prussians barely a year ago had been received in Dresden with much rejoicing, as if he had been the glorious winner of the war.

'Here you have, dear Friedrich, an example of the human attitude of our Saxons who irrespective of any intellectual or political convictions do their best to answer the question, how can I in times like these support my family and myself in the best possible way.'

Friedrich answered, 'You may be right here. But at least when receiving the King I would have expected a bit more reserve on the side of the Dresdeners. Have they forgotten or never realized that the King by his fluctuating attitude and his persistent adherence to Napoleon has caused great harm to his country? More than half of the state is lost, and what is worse, also a large part of the population. I will never forget what ridiculous byzantinism the population in Dresden displayed when our prince elector was made King in 1806, and, nota bene, by the hand of a foreign ruler. The *rector magnificus* of the university did not consider it silly to put up the following slogan over the doors of the anatomy building: 'Even the dead call out: Long live the King.'

Admittedly there were some few who gathered under the slogan:

'Vivat, Friedrich August is King,

Hide the gold to which you wish to cling.'

But there were enough servile people around the King who prevented him from hearing about this.'

'What do you expect of people,' Gottlieb replied. 'The dynasty of the Wettins, having ruled for centuries, was for many the only reliably stable factor left in those turbulent times after the people's trust in the allies was thoroughly shaken by the division.'

Friedrich did not answer at once but cut himself a bite of meat and ate it with a piece of bread and a carrot. Then he sampled the white wine that Gottlieb had poured for him from the pitcher on the table. He sighed and looked gratefully at Gottlieb and his wife.

'Oh, how good it is, a rich warm meal with the excellent Meissen wine.'

'Eat and drink, dear Friedrich, there is still much left.' Frau Gottlieb nodded to him kindly. She and the children had water.

Friedrich said: 'Looking at the situation more closely, I should not lament Saxony's loss of land and people. What we wish for is a unified Germany without all those borders and restrictions. So, in the end it might even be advantageous if land and people go to Prussia, which has done so much more for the German nation than Saxony. But what I said about the King I will stand by.'

The pastor did not comment on this remark, because he did not want to start a discussion about the King and his politics in the presence of his wife and children.

When they had all finished eating the dessert of preserved pears and the children had already begun shifting their behinds restlessly on their chairs, Gottlieb said grace and everyone stood up.

'If your time allows let's go to my study,' Gottlieb said to his guest. 'Our talk about Ramdohr and the art critics is not finished yet. And my dear wife will certainly bring us a cup of hot coffee.'

Frau Gottlieb and their guest agreed, and so the two friends went to the pastor's office, where they sat on two leather-covered chairs at a small side table.

CHAPTER 10

The office was a cozy study that corresponded nicely with the character of its possessor. Bookshelves made of smoothly planed and darkened wood lined the walls and reached to the low ceiling.

A refectory table, which had found its way from the old monastery to the vicarage, stood under the small windows the openings of which revealed the thickness of the stonework.

Now with the high May sun shining, the room was warm and tolerably bright. In the corner next to the door there was a big iron stove, its lower half made of tiles, which could be fired from the hall.

The heavy table was covered with books and writing instruments. Prior to meeting Friedrich in the cathedral, the pastor had worked on his sermon for the coming Sunday. It was Rogate, named after the Gospel of John, the gospel of the right way of praying. The pastor wanted to preach about the first epistle of Paul to Timothy, Chapter 2, 1-6. Above all he wanted to make plain the importance of the first two verses: 'I exhort therefore, that, first of all, supplications, prayers, intercessions, and giving of thanks be made for all men; for kings and for all that are in authority; that we may lead a quiet and peaceable life in all godliness and honesty.'

These admonitions were particularly dear to Gottlieb, being weary of the political turmoil and hysterics of the past years. So much had overwhelmed the people, so many had lost relatives, friends and belongings that they now yearned for an untroubled life under the firm rule of a royal house deeply rooted in history.

Most wanted to take up their rightful place in society, wanted to know who was above, who was under and who was among them, and in this way lead a godly life since the rules for what was allowed and what was forbidden depended on the recognition of an undisturbed social order ordained by God.

Among the chorals suggested by Gottlieb was 'Give peace, O Lord, in our time because there is no one else to fight for us and help us from our misery'. He thought that after the long period of wars the yearning for peace resided deep in the hearts of the people and would unite them in hope and confidence.

Filled with these thoughts the pastor had almost forgotten his guest, which Friedrich did not seem to mind. He stood before his oil painting *The Chasseur in the Forest,* hanging to the right of the door in good light. As he studied it the pastor stepped to his side.

'I hope you don't look disapprovingly, dear friend', he said. 'You have by your talent and without betraying your peculiar style, manifested your patriotic conviction. And there was hardly a visitor at the art exhibition who was not moved by it.'

'Yes,' Friedrich replied, 'the painting is a parable on the doom of Napoleon's Grand Army in Russia.'

Gottlieb responded with animation. 'Halting his step, the straggling French soldier listens to the silence of the woods, and the viewer can feel the hopeless fear that descends upon him, evil and threatening, with the approach of nightfall. And independent of the patriotic content, you, Friedrich, through the use of that specific coloring have grasped an aspect of nature in winter that bodes no good for the man. And impressive, how the small figure of the soldier in front of the tremendous vastness of the forest helps the observer to enter into the landscape.'

Friedrich, despite his usual reserve, was, like all artists, very receptive to praise, especially if it was so expertly worded and corresponded so perfectly with the intentions he had when painting the picture.

Gottlieb had by now talked himself into a great enthusiasm.

'And the French chasseur is not just a lost and lonely figure but a part of the usurper's army looking at a well-deserved fate. He is also a human being, our brother—and in this sense he is not small at all—who arouses our compassion and also our respect as he bravely tries to face his fate alone and proud. He gazes ahead in readiness, till carrying his sword in order to be able to defend himself if necessary. But his doom seems certain, indicated by the bird of death on the tree stump in the foreground. To stand in a thoughtful and dignified manner when faced with such hopelessness deserves our respect.'

The pastor fell silent and took his eyes slowly from the picture.

Then Friedrich said, 'I as the painter permit myself a completely individual form of expression, which constitutes, in my eyes, the very nature of art. At the same time, I must allow the viewer to perceive my works according to his own understanding. And so, an unpolitical person may see this picture as a landscape with a soldier who went for a walk in the winter forest and will soon join his comrades in their camp, scaring away the raven from its tree stump, and then returning to his homeland after retreating as ordered.'

Gottlieb agreed with the painter and continued by talking about the nature of art.

'From this we can conclude that there are infinitely different paths leading toward art, and surely the venerated old masters were aware of this. So, it is wrong that our arrogant art critics put them before us as examples that must blindly be followed for all time.'

At this moment the door opened and Frau Gottlieb brought in a steaming pot of coffee, two cups and a plate with Leipzig Larks. Gottlieb did not mind the interruption, being fond of this marzipan pastry which he had gotten to know as a studiosus theologiae at Leipzig. The name of the pastry had a peculiar origin. The songbird after which it was named was roasted with herbs and eggs and served as filling in a pastry crust. A Saxon king eventually banned the hunting of the birds because they were believed to be important for agriculture. So, the clever Saxons replaced the meat-filled pastry with the sweet version thus preserving the tradition of the Leipzig Lark while no longer killing the birds.

In Frau Gottlieb's version, she made a dough from flour, sugar, butter, eggs and milk and let it rest in the cool cellar overnight. For the marzipan filling she slowly heated crushed almonds and confectioner' sugar in a pot. Stirring continuously, she added a few spoonfuls of rum and a small amount of cinnamon.

In the meantime, Ilse, the maid, rolled out the dough to half an inch thickness, cut out rounds and pressed them into small tins, not more than half full. Then Frau Gottlieb put the marzipan on the dough with two stripes crosswise on top, after which the larks were baked golden brown. 'They are best when eaten still warm,' remarked Reverend Gottlieb after he and his guest had served themselves. 'You need a lot of hot coffee to go with them, because the larks are dry and sweet. In this way,' God's servant added, 'one gift of God necessitates another one and makes the world more bearable.'

His wife, already on her way to the door, turned to her husband and said: 'Into these two gifts of God, as well as into today's lunch, for which you have thanked God, I and Ilse have put quite a lot of work and time. May I squeeze out a bit of your thanks for us?'

The pastor blushing visibly, went up to his wife, embraced her, kissed her on the forehead and said, 'You know, my love, how much I treasure what you contribute to my work for our parish. If you, and of course Ilse, did not do the lion's share of the work in the household and the garden as well as for the education of our children I wouldn't know how to fulfill my office as required.'

Now it was Frau Gottlieb's turn to blush. She kissed her husband on the cheek and left the room. She thought how much, after so many years of married life, she still loved him and how in moments like these she felt a warm and also painful yearning. When young, she had thought love got its exquisite edge from an awareness of its transience. Now she felt that real love was characterized by its permanence, and that it was youth that was fleeting.

Friedrich had observed the little scene with interest. He had not expected such a direct comment from Frau Gottlieb. So this is what it is like to be married, he thought. Obviously, one must be careful with some things. Once they are married, wives are not only housekeepers and bed mates. They also want attention in quite a different way. He would keep this little experience in mind, and, if the time should prove propitious, use it to his betterment.

His host turned to the coffee table and encouraged his guest to partake. Friedrich, who regarded the frugal life he was leading as a form of existence befitting man and artist alike, still ate and drank with gusto. Emptying his cup, he said:

'Truly, Chamberlain von Ramdohr would have remained silent if I had with my *Cross in the Mountains* followed without deviation the example of the famous masters of old. But also here, with my *Chasseur*, I maintain if a picture affects the viewer's soul, if it stirs up his emotion, it has fulfilled the most important function of a work of art, even if it is bad in form, color and execution. If, on the other hand, a picture, well done in form and color, leaves the viewer cold, without feeling, then it is not a true work of art but just a finely done artificiality.'

'This, my dear Friedrich, seems to be a very extreme opinion,' Gottlieb replied, 'because a precondition for awakening the described emotion in the viewer certainly is the painting's masterly execution. This can easily be seen in your painting. And so, my contention is that the idea the artist intends to express should be painted in the best possible harmony with his skill as a painter. And, by the way, this harmony shows itself in *The Chasseur* through the perfectly depicted aura of the lost dream.

Now imagine this painting as having been done badly in form and color. You don't think, do you, it would have had the effect, would have brought forward the emotion that you intended?'

Friedrich wanted to say something, but decided to remain silent, because he felt that on the one hand the pastor had good arguments, and on the other hand that he had for lack of the right words not succeeded in putting into speech what he felt was the core of his art. And so, he preferred to say nothing, because often the essential things were lost if one tried to put them into words. And also, not only art is no man's servant, but having an opinion and talking about it openly is the right of everybody.

After remaining a while together enjoying their mutual company, Friedrich stood up to start on his way home. The clock on the tower of St. Afra struck 4. Reverend Gottlieb saw his guest to the door and wished him a safe journey home. His friend would take the 5 o'clock stage coach to Dresden.

PART 3
DRESDEN, MAY 1816

CHAPTER 11

Some days later, early in the morning, Christian August Silberschlag and Caspar David Friedrich met at the entrance of the court theater in Dresden for a long walk. Silberschlag had returned from London and his travels through the whole of Britain a few weeks earlier and had spent some time in Berlin, where he had delivered his report to Karl Friedrich Schinkel. He had related his experiences and the result of his inquiries about English landscape painting. Then, once more in Dresden, he had carefully and repeatedly embraced his dear Johanna, who had whispered to him, her father being within hearing distance, that Dr Carus had assured her that everything was in order with the child growing under her heart, and its birth would in all likelihood happen without complications at the end of July.

Since Friedrich loved the dawning of the day as much as dusk and the night, he had arranged to meet his friend at six o'clock in the morning. That had not been easy for Silberschlag, who would have liked to stay in bed longer and enjoy the warm bed and the soft arms of his wife.

From the court theater they went to the Augustus bridge and from there looked eastward, towards the sunrise. A dense morning fog still lay on the Elbe, and the last stars were fading in the sky. It was cold, but the dew on the Elbe meadows promised another warm and sunny day.

Their walk had been planned quite some time ago. First of all, Friedrich, who through his lonely wanderings at night and his activity as a guide for foreigners knew the city quite well, wanted to show and explain to his friend, who had moved to Dresden much later than Friedrich, the most interesting sights. His occasional work as a guide had helped him earn a living when his painting and drawing did not bring in much money. Silberschlag could add what he had read about the city and at the same time talk about his journey to London.

Above the bridge the river curved away so that they could not see very far. To the right rose the spire of the Church of Our Lady with its magnificent dome, its orb and cross, almost three hundred feet into the morning sky. Friedrich, who did not like baroque architecture, could not but admire the accomplishment of the city architect George Bähr. He had been the city council master carpenter, and had designed the church, which was made of sandstone, some eighty years previously. The great spire dominated the townscape, and the Dresdeners regarded themselves lucky that the bombardment by the Prussians had not destroyed it in AD 1760 as had happened to the main church of the city, the Church of the Holy Cross.

What Friedrich, and with him Silberschlag, the latter undoubtedly influenced by Karl Friedrich Schinkel, did not like about Baroque architecture was the contradiction of its playful and worldly embellishments to its mission of leading man straight to heaven. This style did not service the goal of worship like Gothic, but satisfied a human and earthly desire, the wish for drama, movement, tension and abundance of emotions, all of which the painter aesthetically opposed. But still, the Church of Our Lady deserved some admiration.

As they viewed the church, the first rays of the sun struck the golden cross and the dome.

'It is so sad,' Silberschlag said, 'that Bähr did not live to see the completion of his greatest work. The building was finished in 1740, when he had already been dead for two years.'

'But at least he reached the ripe age of 72,' Friedrich answered, 'an age which we might wish for one day. Rumor has it that he died from the fall off the scaffolding, or even jumped from it. Hardly believable. Does one, at that age, climb up a scaffold? But still, it might be easier to leave this world after having nearly accomplished such a work.'

'Yes, a real miracle it is,' said Silberschlag. 'And I think it is just a rumor, completely unproven, that he fell or jumped from the scaffold. The truth is he suffered from suffocative catarrh and consumption. And the continual criticism of his decisions, frictions with the royal, municipal and clerical authorities, and the drudgery of the work were contributing factors. He was also plagued by worries concerning his six underage children, three daughters and three sons. One can only hope that he did not suffer much before dying. He may have been helped to a peaceful death by what people said was his profound faith and the satisfaction with his architectural miracle. In Berlin Schinkel spoke approvingly of Bähr and his church. In sharp contrast with the excesses of other architects, Schinkel had said, Bähr was not so much interested in technical virtuosity and playful distractions, but had aimed at the artistic solution of an architectural problem. He wanted to erect a domed church that provided for the needs of a large Protestant congregation. At the same time, it was to be solid, which meant made of stone, not wood, including the cupola. The majority of the experts had been against Bähr's daring design, among them Chiary, the builder of the Catholic Church of the Royal Court, though he was a great master of tower construction himself. Only Bähr's third design was accepted in 1726, but at the last moment the authorities wanted the so-called lantern of the dome made of timber for fear the pillars would not carry the weight of stone. All this Schinkel knew from a kind of literary biography of Bähr, which was published here in Dresden and found its way to Berlin. It is a pity, Schinkel had said, that he forgot the name of the biographer. He had added that the city council members were not quite mistaken in their doubts about the cupola. According to what Schinkel had learned, the weight of the cupola was more than 12,000 tons, and the architect should have tried to divert part of this enormous load from the supporting pillars to the outer walls.'

'Be that as it may,' Friedrich commented, 'in any case the significance of this building, however it adorns the silhouette of the city, lies in the way it is constructed.'

'Yes,' Silberschlag replied, 'as Schinkel would say, the construction must serve the function. And in the case of this church, it does so to a high degree. Eight slender, radially positioned pillars carry the inner cupola, which opens to the lofty dome. This rests on the outer walls, and the four stair towers in the corners form their main abutments. Large arch-openings are to be found in the lower line of the cupola so that even at this height there is still room for galleries. Thus, the best possible use is made of the space, because these galleries and loggias are in fact seven stories. This is how Schinkel in Berlin described the Church of Our Lady to me, though he did not tell me when he had visited it. Or perhaps he had commissioned someone to describe it to him.'

'The building's functionality was put to the test in a truly ungodly way, certainly not foreseen by George Bähr, when the sandstone cupola needed to withstand the Prussian bombs in 1760. They bounced off it without doing damage.'

'Here can be seen,' said Silberschlag, 'how rarely the hopes of the people are fulfilled. In 1726 the Dresdnischen Merckwürdigkeiten newspaper reported what a copper chest containing a copy of the Augsburg Confession, which Emperor Charles V had been handed by the Protestants on the imperial diet in Augsburg in 1530, had been buried in the foundation. The Confession was intended to facilitate an understanding between Catholics and Protestants. This was supplemented with a message from the town council, which started with the heart-felt words: 'There is peace, thanks be to Almighty God, in our country as well as in the Roman Empire and the whole of Europe.' And look how soon all hopes for a lasting peace were destroyed.'

The friends fell silent for a while. Then Silberschlag continued: 'But despite all his daring, wrote Bähr's unknown biographer, 'he did not with all his architectural mastership, meet the needs of his time. The massive solidity of Bähr's creation did not satisfy the public's desire for gallantry.'

'O yes,' Friedrich said, 'the needs of the times. What are they, and who determines this spirit of the time? And how far is one prisoner of this spirit without knowing it, and how far can one escape from it? Or put it this way: Does time make man, or man time? Probably the former, because even the greatest genius cannot overcome his time or its spirit. And should a rare genius succeed in this, the contemporary world will not understand it, but will say he is out of his mind, and only posterity will recognize him as one of theirs. But because he works in his time and for his contemporaries, he would like this to happen a bit earlier, at least enough to make a living.'

With this they crossed over the bridge and came into the Neustadt, which had been called Altendresden three quarters of a century earlier.

The Neustadt market with the statue of Augustus the Strong was already becoming busy. The copper-beaten and fire gilded statue portrayed the prince elector and king in an imposing attitude on a rearing horse and looking eastward.

In its shadow, vendors opened their booths, and carts drawn by strong heavy horses rumbled over the cobblestones in order to supply the city with the necessary provisions and goods together with the cargo barges on the Elbe. Hawkers in their open stalls prepared to sell vegetables, sauerkraut, pickled herrings, flour, salt, sago and spices. Butchers and bakers from surrounding regions and suburbs likewise offered their products for the day. The first maids and cooks were to be seen, most of whom belonged to the court officials, nobles, merchant, teachers, doctors and goldsmiths living at the Neumarkt.

Housewives were a rare sight, however, and if seen, were always accompanied by their maids, who carried the shopping baskets. For women of the higher classes it was not considered proper to go out alone. Friedrich saw their lace-trimmed bonnets, without which no woman would appear, and he thought what his future wife might look like. She would certainly also wear a wide crinoline with a hoop of fishbone in it. It was interesting for the painter to see how even small differences in social standing and age expressed themselves in how they were dressed, and he remarked on this to his companion.

The sun in the meantime had risen and began to warm the paving. Sparrows and pigeons hopped about among the booths in search of feed.

Friedrich quickened his steps and urged Silberschlag to do likewise.

'It was good,' said the latter, 'that the evil foe Napoleon had ordered the destruction of the city's fortifications anno 9 so that now we can really enjoy all the beautiful sights unhindered by walls and ramparts. Now the city can spread out and free itself from the narrowness of the middle ages.'

'You are right, friend, but his motives were certainly not those of city beautification. Let's now walk through Grosse Meissnerstrasse to the Japanese Palace.'

Now it was Silberschlag's turn, and he could, not without a certain pride, convey his newly acquired knowledge to his friend.

'In its original form it was called Holland Palace when it was still in the possession of Count Flemming, who later sold it to the King. Flemming, who had supported the prince elector in his desire to become Polish king, to the detriment of Saxony, I believe, was a man of little talent but just enough to know how to dominate the King, just as Count Brühl later dominated Augustus III.'

'Good that you are saying this. It reminds us of how the ups and downs of political life can affect the fate of a city, even of a whole country. Without Flemming's assistance Poland's crown would perhaps never have been acquired by the prince elector and so would not have brought damage to the country. As it happened, the House of Wettin, Albertine line, ceased being Protestant and so came into new conflict with Brandenburg's Hohenzollern, who then without doubt, and let me add happily, grew to be the leader of the Protestants of the Empire.'

Silberschlag had waited for a chance to continue with his talk on the Japanese Palace.

'Anyway, it was here that Augustus the Strong planned to realize his dream of creating a 'porcelain palace'. The roofs, the interior décor, in fact practically everything was to be made of porcelain. After he had purchased the building in 1717, he commissioned the leading Dresden architects Pöppelmann, de Bodt, Longuelune and Knöffel with the conversion work. With its architectural sculptures in state-of-the-art 'chinoiserie' style and its Japanese curved roofs, the four-wing complex was one of the masterpieces of the

Dresden Baroque. However, the full-scale vision of the 'porcelain palace' was never completed.'

'You are telling me this, Silberschlag, as if I didn't know it, and as if I wouldn't be maddened anew every time by the craving of our Germans for the foreign. Our painters travel to Italy. My brother goes to France and does not recognize the danger still lurking there, the danger that people believe everything could be done using reason, forgetting that above plain reason there has to be the rule of conscience.

Reason, dear Silberschlag, is the analytical and logical working of the intellect. Conscience in its highest spiritual sense includes the holy and deep belief in the existence of a higher truth.

I had to ask my brother, who was in Lyon as a journeyman in Napoleon's time, to stop writing me letters as long as he was in France. His stay there hurt my feelings too much.'

Silberschlag, who did not share the painter's stubborn anti-French attitude and was more inclined to side with Goethe with regard to France and Napoleon, preferred not to comment on Friedrich's last remarks.

They crossed the Elbe over the Marienbrücke in a kind of tense silence, passed the Little Ostra Enclosure, went upriver until they reached Brühl's Terrace. Both felt the tension that had arisen between them and gave each other time to overcome it and return to their old level of intimacy. They went down the staircase leading to the Zeughausplatz and sat down at a table that stood half in the shade. Silberschlag did not forget to say that the construction of this open staircase had been ordered by Prince Repnin, the Russian Governor General.

CHAPTER 12

'Now, Silberschlag, tell me about your great journey. And you have certainly raised my curiosity about Turner. Your dear wife, to be honest, occasionally read to me from your letters, of course only paragraphs relating to the well-known painter.'

Here, as they sat at a table in front of an inn they were interrupted by the innkeeper, who had come to take their orders. Both had slices of bread and butter and small radishes, which were raised on hotbeds under glass in the innkeeper's garden and were available already in May. For drinks they asked for a large pitcher of water. The landlord, an art enthusiast who regularly visited the academic art exhibitions in Brühl's Picture Gallery, was familiar with Friedrich as a painter, and to show his admiration, brought them several chunks of Thuringian cheese, which he regularly received in large vats from his brother's farm near Neustadt on the Orla in the Grand Duchy of Saxony-Weimar.

The friends began eating with good appetite, and Silberschlag enjoyed the dark, hefty bread, which he had missed during his visit to London.

Friedrich awaited his younger friend's report not without a certain inner agitation. He knew himself well enough to admit that, when other artists were praised, he was not free from jealousy or even envy, and to make amends for this unhealthy trait of character he tended to take up the praise and amplify it—though with a guilty conscience. Should another painter be criticized, he contradicted the critic, thus often succeeding in provoking an even harsher criticism. On such occasions he would attempt to control his feelings, because he knew they were not befitting.

Silberschlag for his part was well aware that speaking to one artist, whom he highly estimated, about another artist, whom he likewise admired, was a delicate situation. Not wanting to hurt one nor to do the other an injustice, he decided to tread carefully. Besides, he knew Friedrich and his desire for what the English called fairness, which would make it easier for him to give an unbiased account.

'Where do I begin, considering the vast amount of impressions I have had in the past half year?'

'Tell me about Turner and his art. We will find time later for everything else.'

In the meantime, the sun stood high in the sky, and when they looked up, they could see the golden cross on the dome of the Church of Our Lady. The inn had become quite busy, and several people were sitting on the benches around them enjoying the fare.

'I believe,' Silberschlag began, 'that the present English landscape painting differs quite distinctly, I could even say fundamentally, from the German. On one side, the English side, we observe a pragmatism that does not care about spiritual or philosophical matters, but depicts what the eye sees and mind or intellect confirms. On the other, the German side, as you, friend Friedrich know best and I, to be honest, feel unworthy to say, have joined what people like to call the

German character, which is religion and politics, where the landscapes serve as symbols, and where a mere subjective kind of serenity without any ideological considerations is not what the painter aims at. In fact, German painters, and you above all, dear friend, set up a visual conundrum: a sense that there is more to the scene you are looking at than can be quite grasped. I would like to call it a kind of transcendental method.'

'Are you saying. Silberschlag, that the English or rather Turner, don't care about the consequences of their art?'

'No, not at all. What I mean is that the dissatisfaction of the Germans with the present, the resulting yearning for the past, which they imagine was better, and for nature, and their craving to always get to the bottom of things—in which they can never reach a satisfying result—instead of accepting their fate and making the best of it ...' Here Silberschlag faltered and paused to gather his thoughts.

'What I want to say is that all this often leads to a sad and strained attitude, sometimes inexplicably connected with a guilty conscience, that invades the actual artistic expression. And in England, it is exactly the opposite.'

Friedrich drank water from his earthen cup, poured some for Silberschlag and indicated that he might continue.

'Turner takes not the least bit of interest in religion, and the only things that interest him in the bible seem to be the apocalypse and the plagues of Egypt.

Regarding his method of painting, my impression is that he is the first artist to perceive light as color and color as light and transfers this perception into painting. Traditionally, light was regarded as a transparent medium that makes objects visible and reveals their color to the viewer. Turner looks at it as a dynamic force that acts on the objects being viewed, penetrates them and disperses them into colors.'

Here he was interrupted by Friedrich, who had become uneasy when hearing these last words.

'This sounds rather odd to me. What you are saying sounds as if the light in Turner's paintings becomes independent, is no longer serving to illuminate the painter's perception of the world, but becomes itself the subject of the painting.'

'I agree,' answered Silberschlag, 'when viewing some of his works I had a similar impression. And it is exactly what a number of his critics reproach him with. But he simply looks at nature differently from us, namely not as something static but as an active process, changing constantly and in permanent dialogue with man. And with all respect, dear Friedrich, remember your Monk at the Sea. Did you not in this painting, as with Cross Beside the Baltic allow light to play a role that captured viewers in such a way that the overall message was forgotten?'

'No, friend, this view seems to me to be not quite right. In Cross Beside the Baltic, and here more than elsewhere, the full moon symbolizing Christ casts a mild light on the cross and the sea. The gray color of the water, I hope, forms a gentle contrast to the colors of the sky. So you see that the light is a means to an end and not an independent object of the picture.'

'No doubt I must submit to a more competent judgment,' Silberschlag responded and continued, 'It is understandable that Turner is subjected, to put it mildly, to the bewildered astonishment of his colleagues and the art critics. Particularly after the first public exhibition of Snowstorm. Hannibal Crossing the Alps the hostility tempered with some praise has grown strongly. He is crazy, it is rumored, has ill eyes and suffers from a color vision impairment, which they are unable to describe adequately.'

Friedrich listened thoughtfully. Through Silberschlag's choice of words and the meaning he attached to them, Friedrich dimly sensed a future he could not quite grasp.

That Turner's ideas and methods were different from his own way of painting was clear, but it seemed to point to a future that he, Friedrich, did not want.

Still, he felt a greater nearness to the Englishman than their paintings suggested since his pictures were becoming increasingly misunderstood and rejected, and fewer people seemed to be interested in him. He thought of other things they had in common. Both were about the same age, and Turner, as Friedrich had learned from Silberschlag's letters to his wife, had lost an eight-year-old sister, as Friedrich had lost a brother and sister. And both of them kept a certain distance from the princely courts, and their sovereigns, a position that did not exactly help their careers.

Silberschlag was quiet while his friend sat brooding. Friedrich's sudden and unexplained silences in the middle of a conversation happened quite frequently, and Silberschlag had learned to respect them.

They both felt they had talked enough for the day.

After summoning the innkeeper and paying the bill, Silberschlag said, 'A last word about Turner. How he lets light take effect in his paintings is not without consequences for how he depicts the world. It seems as if he resists the common practice of representation, a spreading realism which in his eyes, as he said to me, grasps the phenomena well enough, but not the essence of things. In this way, by canceling the validity of visible relationship within the composition, he turns away from artistic tradition. Already with his Hannibal the viewer senses the vivid picture structure as being largely in motion. I want to say that in Turner's paintings the scenes that are meant to envelop the viewer no longer seem to occupy a fixed location but appear to dissipate into a vaster firmament. At least a beginning is made, and who knows where this method of painting, which I would like to refer to as a kind of open structure painting determined by light and color will lead Turner.'

'I thank you very much for your revelations,' Friedrich said, 'though I cannot quite follow your last words. When the objects no longer have a fixed place in a painting, as you are indicating, then the painter abandons what I would call his proper job. Where shall this lead us? To a mere presentation of a colored impression?

But let us stop here. The best explanations, and I must say you did your best to explain Turner to me, cannot replace personal acquaintance. I suppose it will still be a while, and may not happen at all, that I can have a look at one of Turner's works. And he will not see one of mine. You wrote that he is widely traveled, and has been to Germany, Switzerland, France and Italy. With this I cannot compete, which I honestly do not regret. I simply cannot travel away, particularly not with a companion. I must remain alone and know that I am alone in order to take nature in and enter it deeper and feel it more completely with every visit. I must devote myself to my clouds and rocks and trees and dawns and dusks in order to be what I am. Solitude I need for my talk with nature. Once I lived for a whole week in the Uttewalder Grund gorge between rocks and firs, and did not meet a living person the whole time. But I must admit I cannot advise anyone to follow this method—even to me it was almost too much. Inadvertently gloom begins spreading in one's soul. But I must be alone in familiar surroundings. I confess I avoid foreign or new impressions because I fear I would no longer be what I am.'

Friedrich was silent after this confession which was uncustomary for this usually reserved man. Silberschlag, uncertain about how to respond felt a desire to put his hand on the painter's arm and comfort him in his dark isolation, though he did not dare.

Friedrich gathered himself and, returning to Turner, said, 'Maybe one day he will come to Dresden, or at least nearer to it than just to the Rhine and Moselle.'

'This may well be,' said Silberschlag. 'And should Herr Schinkel in Berlin decide to purchase paintings from Turner for the King, one will at least be able to see his works. But I have my doubts. His Majesty the Prussian King would certainly prefer your paintings to Turner's, I'm quite sure of that.'

Then the friends said good-bye to each other, and Friedrich made for home, while Silberschlag started on his way to

Justice Councilor von Globig, whose sons he taught conversational English. Von Globig was the court official who together with the Count of Schulenburg had signed the treaty with Prussia at the end of the Wars of Liberation against Napoleon. This treaty determined that the Saxon King 'for eternal times for Himself and all descendants and successors renounced all demands on the provinces hereafter mentioned in favor of His Majesty the King of Prussia.'

These provinces comprised half of Saxony with 57,8% of its population. The division was still the cause of much resentment among the Saxon people, which was directed against the allies. And it was also the reason why they pitied and respected their King, who was so deeply humiliated by the allies.

In the house of the Justice Councilor, through talks with him, Silberschlag had been able to take note of the political and diplomatic developments in Saxony and to keep himself in the political picture.

CHAPTER 13

A messenger brought the long-awaited letter. After receiving it Friedrich offered the man a glass of water, but being in a hurry, the messenger refused it and departed.

Friedrich sat down on the wooden bench on the forecourt beside the stairs, broke the seal and took out the document. From a friend, he already knew what the letter would be about.

Fine, now he was a member of the Dresden academy. And was promised a yearly salary of - hard to believe—150 thalers. Would they one day make him a professor, he asked himself, with permission to teach students?

He had some doubts. In the eyes of the authorities he was not what they called academic enough and did not fit into their conventional framework. The Ramdohrs of this world would howl if students were to be exposed to his teaching.

He leaned against the doorjamb and closed his eyes. Odd, how good fortune is so often bittersweet. He had not felt like painting for some time and had to force himself to take up the brush for even a single stroke. And then the talk with Silberschlag about Turner had made him uneasy. Now the membership in the academy had come, which for such a long time he had so ardently desired, and instead of making him happy it dampened his mood in regard to the faint prospect of teaching.

But there was nothing he could do. He had to go on working and must not allow himself to give way to current sentiment and opinion. Not long ago he had been inordinately praised; now the same people criticized him inordinately. But as he had accepted the adulation he would now live with the criticism. But it was odd that he was now disparaged for what he had once been praised. They, whoever they were, the public, the critics and colleagues, claimed they were simply responding to the times while he, the artist, stuck in the past.

Friedrich rose and went into his poorly equipped studio. Contrary to expectation, it was not bright. Rather, one window was covered with black paper, and half of the other window had been blocked by the lower shutter, thus creating something like dusk. On the easel stood a stretched canvas and before it was placed a chair. Friedrich approached the painting. Although it was almost finished, he had not touched it for weeks, though it urgently demanded completion.

As was his habit, he had not started to paint until the picture was fully realized in his imagination, and only after the creative spirit drove him to it. He started by drawing with chalk, then continued with pencil until finally, when he found it good enough, commenced with brush and oil to complete it.

He had decided upon a title for it even before he had started painting: Two Men by the Sea at Moonrise.

God is everywhere in Nature, and he had tried to make it visible to those who were able to see it. For others, it was merely the sea, the moon and two men.

But anyone who has eyes to see, sees: The men in the painting wear Altdeutsche Tracht, the German National Costume which, in the people's mind, was as an indication of their patriotic convictions. In 1814 had not Ernst Moritz Arndt in his publication 'On Custom, Fashion and Costume' recommended, not to say ordered, all German patriots to wear this garment? For men it consisted of a gray or black frock coat, buttoned up to the collar, over which a broad shirt collar was laid; the hair was long and hung down to the shoulders and was covered with a black velvet beret; a black cape completed the costume. For women Arndt had strongly recommended a long high-waisted dark dress with long sleeves and high-necked collar.

Friedrich studied his painting. The two wanderers had ventured to the two farthest rocks in the water in order to contemplate the rising moon. Their heads are silhouetted against the horizon and thus form a connection between beach, sea and sky. The moon stands between them, and the stones and clouds are arranged so that a mood is created which expresses a calm immersion in what is being viewed. The gentle movement of the waves can hardly be seen. The relationships in the composition, near and far, worldliness and otherworldliness, men and moon, are separate on the surface but all of them the painter wants to be understood as a symbol of Christ, and therefore they are unified and thus connected.

Friedrich thought of how, in Silberschlag's account, Turner often relied on chance when composing his pictures. Can one really paint like that, without plan, in the end without

God? Does not one owe it to God to transfer His enormous design of creation and salvation into the painting on the basis of a plan? Of course, this presupposes the belief that God manifests Himself everywhere, in nature and the entire universe.

The figures in the scenery stand on boulders, separated, nothing seeming to connect them. But the stones are symbols of faith. That is to say they have a distinct reference point in the infinity of God's world, at last in a connection to the otherworld.

And this is what his critics do not like. Symbols of faith in a landscape painting, is this allowed? For them nature is something heathen, remote from God, and therefore does not belong in an altarpiece, as Christian symbols are not supposed to exist in nature—this he had had to experience painfully.

In the sky the clouds are like gables. This had been his way too, as with the Tetschen Altar, to adapt shapes found in nature to forms created by man. Truly, for someone with eyes to see this means that nature as a whole is a place imbued with the presence of God, that it is His church.

The painter stepped back in order to view the picture in its completeness. He felt he had succeeded here, as in no other work, in expressing with the greatest clarity, his understanding of faith. Yes, he could leave it as it was. He must stop trying to touch it up and improve it, an old and sometimes detrimental habit. And also, he would then never be finished with it.

The following night the painter had a dream whose torments pursued him all the next day.

He had hardly gone to bed near midnight, and covered himself with a woolen blanket, when he fell asleep and began dreaming.

In a cold black torrent of water he found himself swimming behind his dead brother, who in this dream was a fully-grown man. They swam against the current, which broadened into a lake reflecting the stars. His brother stopped before a huge wall of ice, which towered into the night sky.

Suddenly he could see his brother no longer and called his name. When his brother reappeared a huge ice bear emerged from the water and began biting him on the neck and pushing him under. What could Friedrich do? If he swam near to help, the bear would let go of this brother and kill him instead. So in an agony of guilt, he turned and swam away faster and faster, while behind him his brother cried out in pain.

When he reached the bank, a group of girls were sitting there. Climbing out of the water he saw that he was naked. Desperately he tried to cover himself and hide from the girls, who stared at him, pointing and nudging each other. Covering himself with his hands, he ran away, whereupon he woke up.

The moon shone through the window in his chamber. Looking around, he saw that he had gone to bed in the coat he normally wore when painting, and under which he was usually bare. The coat had opened, the blanket had fallen on the floor and he lay exposed.

Hastily, holding the coat together with his hands, he got up from the bed and went into his studio, stopping by the window.

The moon shone peacefully on the sleeping town, and his heart was calmed. With this recurring dream of loss, guilt and failure, which was to come again and again, he would have to live. Winter, death, and the hereafter would be the background against which he would have to paint until he himself went down to the grave.

PART 4
LONDON, ST. JAMES'S PALACE, OCTOBER 1814

CHAPTER 14

The King walked up and down in front of the painting, stepped nearer, stepped back again and shook his head. He simply could not come to terms with this Turner, member of his Royal Academy. He should have known since his father had told him how Turner had conducted himself in the Academy in 99.

The 'Democrats' in the Academy, the party Turner had joined, were opposed to the King's 'Court Party', and were determined to maintain the rights of the Academy against the King. What an impudent insubordination. It was after all part of the prerogative of the crown to rule what should happen in its Academy. But no, they believed they must have elections. As if these would necessarily lead to the best choice for a post.

Five years later, in 1804, there was an additional controversy when a new Keeper had to be found. Turner had supported the democrat Smirke, who was regarded as dangerous. This rogue, when Queen Marie Antoinette of France was beheaded, was reported to have said: 'There are more crowned heads for whom the guillotine would be the proper remedy.' All that was a long time ago, but not easily forgotten.

With a scowl on his face, the King poured himself another brandy from the decanter, added a good measure of laudanum, which gave off a pleasant smell of cloves and cinnamon, and drank it at one gulp. He knew that this concoction was not good for him in the long run, but how was he to endure the constant attacks of gout, which were intensified by his corpulence? He had hardly been able to sleep the previous night, and even turning in bed had caused him to cry out in pain.

Besides, when as now he was lingering between numbness and relaxation, it helped him to endure the sight of this painter's sorry effort as well as the imminent weekly visit of his prime minister Lord Liverpool. Though he did not like the Prime Minister, he knew him to be a clever and art-loving man and could, before talking politics, ask him for his opinion about the painting. Since the King had commissioned the picture on the advice of the noble lord, he could now demand a justification for this advice and at the same time tell him what he intended for this painting.

It was normally hanging here in the ante-room of the St. James's Palace under the critical eyes of the court and, more importantly of those who had to do with the navy. It had been commissioned as the last of a series of battle paintings, which were intended to put the rule of the Hanoverians in a beneficial light.

George admitted to himself that this was necessary. As kings the Hanoverians had not always been fortunate. His regency for his insane father and his own accession to the throne five years previously had caused resentment among his subjects and opposition from the newspapers.

It seemed to him that from the very beginning for whatever reasons he had been the target for ridicule and deprecation from journalists and cartoonists. What had he done wrong? What made people, even those at his court, behave toward him like that?

When he was eighteen years old, he had a mistress, the actress 'Perdita' Robinson, a fascinating and beautiful woman, who was married to a much older man, a gambler, a habitual debtor and a drunkard. So, it was hardly surprising that the two young people fell in love. Perdita, as George called her after her part in A Winter's Tale, desired to escape from her miserable marriage, and he, the Prince of Wales, longed for her experienced caresses and her skillful instructions on how to treat women, fondle them and lead them to the highest joys, all things that a young man alone, without practical advice, could not know.

When she fell ill of a rheumatic fever, he had been forced to give her up since she could no longer provide the services for which he had set her up—at a considerable cost, one had to add. Quite understandable, wasn't it? Mrs. Robinson had responded with coaxing and then threats. An ugly newspaper attack ensued. She threatened to publish the prince's letters, and, inevitably, there was talk of blackmail. Eventually the affair was mediated by Lord Malden (who by now was Mrs. Robinson's lover) and the prince's treasurer Colonel George Hotham, who acted for the King; and during September 1781, in exchange for returning the prince's letters, Mrs. Robinson was rewarded with £5000 and the tacit promise of an annuity. As a consequence, his relationship with his father was further damaged. To be honest, it had already been adversely affected by the attempts of the son's political friends to increase the allowance of the crown prince from £50,000 to £100,000 a year, which caused such a storm of public indignation that the coalition government had been on the point of falling. The King was horrified and angrily pronounced—unjustifiably, the prince believed—that so long as the prince remained unmarried, the outrageous idea of granting an income of £100,000 was a shameful squandering of public money besides an encouragement of extravagance. The 21-year-old prince, however, was not conscious of any sense of guilt, since his friends had made him believe he had a rightful claim to this money. And though he had gotten out of this affair relatively lightly, the next adversity stood waiting in the shadows.

The King made a few cautious steps, filled his glass from the decanter again, took a drink and walked to the window. His eyes began to fill with tears when he remembered Maria, his only true and deep love. He had never been able to forget this woman. Maria Fitzherbert was a Catholic and twice widowed. The King vividly remembered how he first saw her and how he had to promise to marry her before she agreed to become his mistress. Of course he knew that there were three acts of Parliament standing in his way: The Act of Settlement of 1701, the Act of Union of 1707, both prohibiting a prince or princess married to a Catholic from succeeding to the throne, and the Royal Marriages Act of 1772 that stipulated that any marriage of a member of the royal family without the consent of the monarch was null and void. Once he was King, however, he believed he would be able to get around these obstacles.

At first Maria declined to marry him. On learning that she was about to travel abroad, he stabbed himself, then sent his surgeon and his Groom of the Stool and two other friends to tell her that he would tear open his bandages unless she came to him. And by God, he murmured to himself, he would have done that.

Finally, she agreed to marry him and he put a ring upon her finger. He had almost gone mad when the ensuing scandal caused by their liaison forced her to flee to the continent, thus leaving him alone. But what could he do, except write her letters, one of them 42 pages long, and beg her to come home? Finally, to his great delight, she returned to London, and there they were secretly married on a dark December day, in Maria Fitzherbert's drawing room in Park Street in 1785. An Anglican priest, who was released from the Fleet prison only after the Prince made good his debts, conducted the marriage ceremony. The Prince had also promised to make him a bishop once he acceded to the throne. Then came their honeymoon, happiest time of his life, in a hiding place on Ham Common near Richmond.

The King wiped his eyes. How could it happen that he had abandoned the love of his life? His debts, yes, they were the cause. By 94 they had risen to £500,000. He had become so desperate that he was compelled to accept the decision of Parliament, which agreed to increase his allowance enabling him to pay his debts, in return for which he had agreed to marry—his marriage to Maria was officially regarded as illegal and invalid—his cousin Caroline, daughter of the duke of Brunswick, boisterous, tactless, talkative and none too clean. An evil tongue had spread the rumor that he had commented on this choice of a queen, favored by his father, with 'one damned German frau is as good as another'. As if he was that tactless.

The King shuddered when he remembered their first encounter. After dutifully embracing her for the first time and inhaling her odor, who could reproach him for withdrawing to the far corner of the room and asking one of his entourage to get him a glass of brandy?

He admitted to himself that his conduct on the wedding night was not really royal in so far as he fell, insensible with drink, into the bedroom fireplace. He did not remember how he got out again. But in the morning—and this should be added to the list of his good deeds and a clear sign of his devotion to his profession as the heir apparent—he had recovered sufficiently to climb into bed with his wife, who gave birth to their daughter Charlotte exactly nine months later, when they were already living apart. For the next twenty-five years the prince, later the King, and his wife attempted to make life as difficult for each other as possible.

To his relief she decamped to Italy in 1814, a rumor that she had given birth to an illegitimate child being spread. In Italy, always watched by his spies—who could blame him for that—she spent her time with a handsome Italian, who was alleged to have slept in communicating rooms or even in the same bed and to have been present when she bathed. George did not care—except that he was careful to file away his agents' observations for later use—so long as she remained on the continent. This changed, when after a regency of ten years he finally ascended to the throne. She suddenly reappeared in London, visibly worn out, to take part in his crowning ceremony despite the efforts of the new King to keep her away. Beside himself with rage, he demanded the government get rid of this woman immediately. She was offered an annuity of £50,000 if she renounced all claims to marriage and titles, but was cheeky enough to continue to sign her letters as 'Caroline, Queen of England'. And how had his unruly subjects responded, which added a new humiliation to the long list already in existence? The queen's arrival became, as the government had feared, the occasion for widespread public rejoicings. She was the focus of many demonstrations, receiving over 350 addresses of support from all sections of the population, many from groups of women who saw her as a symbol of the oppression of their sex. The King knew that all this was not so much in respect for her but simply to show him how unpopular he was. They held him responsible for the bad state of affairs in the kingdom.

Two days after Caroline's arrival the crowd still thronged in the streets. The windows of the nobility were broken and the coach of the Duke of Wellington was hit with stones. It was rumored that in the barracks the soldiers drank the health of only the queen. A revolution was feared, bloodier than the French. Still Parliament and government found the courage to indict Caroline, the aim being to 'declare Her Majesty Caroline Amelia Elisabeth to have forfeited title, prerogatives, rights, privileges and claims of the princess consort of this empire and to dissolve the marriage between His Majesty and the said Queen.'

The King remembered with scorn how badly the government had conducted this trial. The embarrassing spectacle dragged out for months, the reputation of the monarchy was at its lowest, and of course this was blamed on him. The defendant, this impertinent woman, often sat on the gallery to watch her own trial. The House of Lords, with the barest majority, decided for the King so that the government could end the trial Rex vs. Regina. The tumult in the streets continued. Everywhere Caroline was cheered, and people danced and rioted in London. One of her lawyer's friends was said to have quoted a slave of Octavia's, speaking up for his lady against the abuse by Emperor Nero: 'Her vagina is cleaner than his mouth.' The good lord was cautious enough to cite this in Greek.

One final protest against her fate was an attempt she made to force her way into the abbey on coronation day, 20 July 1821, but she was refused entry and was then suddenly jeered by the crowd that had so recently acclaimed her. A few weeks later she was dead.

Remembering all this, the King sighed, feeling uneasy. He could not entirely wash his hands of her early death. And he regretted the epigram he had authored that had become popular the year before her death:

'Most Gracious Queen, we thee implore
To go away and sin no more:
But, if that effort be too great,
To go away at any rate.'

At the time of her death he had been relieved that she could no longer make trouble. But now he was not sure. One day he would have to finally depart from this world, king or no king, bearing a not inconsiderable load of guilt. The more often he was ill and realized his days, too, were numbered, the more he felt death would come as a relief and a respite from the guilt he had tried to ignore but which found its way irresistibly into his conscience.

To improve his gloomy mood, he remembered a visit to Scotland in his second year of rule. There he was received with the enthusiasm that was a king's due. And it was also quite funny. Sir Walter Scott, whose books he esteemed much, had had the honor of making the arrangements for the King's reception. Scott came on the yacht, the 'Royal George', to present the King with a silver Saint Andrew's Cross as a gift from the ladies of Edinburgh. The King asked him to have a glass of brandy with him. After Scott had drunk the King's health, as an exuberant sign of his loyalty to the King, he asked for permission to keep the glass as a remembrance of this great moment. The King agreed, and Scott put the glass in his back pocket. He forgot about it and when he came home, he sat down and suddenly shrieked out as if stung by an adder. His wife made the famous poet let down his trousers and picked the shards out of his behind. During a reception the next day the King took the lady aside and asked her whether her husband had given the glass a place of honor. She told him about the poet's misfortune, which the King listened to with a hearty laugh. Of course, he gave her another glass. O yes, this was a fine state visit to Scotland.

147

He called his valet and ordered him to refill the decanter, then sent him to fetch Lord Liverpool, who had been waiting half an hour for his audience. The King knew that the Lord would be annoyed, but this was what he wanted. He allowed the man to feel his dislike whenever he could without exactly knowing what it was that he found repulsive.

On one side the unhappy war with the unfaithful colonies in America, now calling themselves United States of America, had occurred during his time as Prime Minister, on the other side there was the military triumph over Napoleon.

At the Congress of Vienna, he had heroically and in the end successfully (forgetting about the American so-called United States) fought for the world-wide abolition of slavery. The King was not quite sure whether he should welcome that. Similar was his reaction to Liverpool's efforts to give precedence to merit over birth when filling posts in church and state. Some things the Prime Minister undertook seemed to him to be shortsighted. The monarchic principle, however undermined it had become in England, required steadiness, a precedence of birth before everything else. This principle had ruled in England since Cerdic, King of the Gewisse, having come from the continent in AD 495, founded the ruling dynasty of the West Saxons, as they subsequently became known. In consequence, he was the individual from whom all kings of the West Saxons traced their descent. With the exception of Canute the Great, the Danish foreign ruler, the two Harolds and the Norman William the Conqueror all English kings stemmed from Cedric or were related to him, including the House of Hanover, his House, now reigning in England.

George liked to lose himself in thoughts about the history of the kings of England, thereby regarding himself as an important link in the chain of persons who had so deeply influenced British, European and last but not least world history. Besides, these thoughts gave him a feeling that he would somehow have an ongoing presence after death. This feeling was strengthened when he considered the lasting effect his passion for pictures and architecture would have on his country. A pity that public opinion did not credit him with this, probably because it cost much money. Ungrateful subjects. They should take the time to look around. There was Regent Street in London, designed by the excellent architect John Nash because of his, the Regent's insistence. Windsor Castle had been renovated and rebuilt, and was not every visitor from abroad overwhelmed by the exotic royal pavilion in Brighton with its Chinese and Indian ornaments, also done by Nash?

One could not praise Nash enough considering his ingenious plans for the conversion of The Queen's House into the grandeur of Buckingham Palace. Later, when people would come to view it, they might perhaps finally grasp what they had to thank the King for.

CHAPTER 15

King George woke from his ruminations when there was a knock on the door. After opening it, the valet stepped back and let the Prime Minister in. Liverpool had allowed himself a small revenge by letting the King wait, which the latter did not seem to have noticed, because he did not comment on it. He indicated that the Lord should come nearer. He told him to put down the box with the state papers and view with him the painting The Battle of Trafalgar by William Turner.

'So, my dear Lord,' began the King, 'before we come to state affairs, let us consider the painting and decide what we'll do with it.'

Liverpool noticed the smell of brandy when the King spoke, and he also realized His Majesty may not have bathed recently, judging from his body odor. He was just able to avoid a sigh, this being one of those days when the life of a Prime Minister was not easy. He could suppress his aversion to the King but could hardly avoid being irritated at the time wasted in unnecessary discussion about a painting, which he was certain would now begin. But since this talk could obviously not be avoided, he resolved at least to stick to his opinion about Turner's work as bluntly as possible.

In actual fact he had more urgent business to discuss with the King today. Primarily he had to persuade the King to give up his resistance to the South America politics of George

Canning, the Foreign Secretary. Last year, together with the American president Monroe, Canning had advocated a guarantee for the newly independent republican states in South America. The King saw here again an attempt to damage the monarchic principle and had secretly plotted intrigues against his own foreign minister. The Prime Minister was aware of this but was unable to combat it, because the King had acted through his kingdom of Hanover. As King of Hanover he could not be controlled by the government or parliament in London and so could use his connections and agents there unhindered. That his Foreign Minister Canning believed he did not understand the importance of access to a new and huge market in these South American countries the King was aware. Of course, it had to be admitted that the new market did not so much directly benefit the government of the United Kingdom but rather the rapidly growing industrial and trade enterprises within the country. But the blossoming of these enterprises, Liverpool had tried to explain to the King, meant the blossoming of the kingdom, of course apart from a number of not so important poorer subjects. But history was not concerned with them, or rather only if they died of hunger or died in the King's battles or suffered otherwise.

The King and his prime minister stood in front of the painting at the distance that it required for a thorough scrutiny. Though the Battle of Trafalgar, which had been fought between the English and French west of Cape Trafalgar, Spain, had occurred almost twenty years before, it was as alive as ever in the memory of the English.

A fleet of 33 ships, 18 French and 15 Spanish battled a British fleet of 27 ships under Admiral Horatio Nelson. The French and Spanish lost 20 ships and 10,000 men, of whom half died or were wounded. The English lost not a single ship, and only 1500 men were either killed or wounded. However, Admiral Nelson also died. A sniper from the crow's nest of an enemy ship recognized him by his bright uniform and his medals, which he had so unwisely decided to wear, and he was fatally shot.

The extensive destruction of the French and Spanish fleets meant Napoleon's plans to invade England were forever shattered. This danger had been great and was only surpassed in English history by the attack of the Spanish Armada in the year of 1588, which along with a large army included the enforcers of the Catholic Inquisition and their instruments of torture. Fortunately, the English, with the help of favorable winds, had been able to repel and partly destroy the enemy.

Both events, which had threatened the very existence of Britain remained in the public memory and were celebrated in lavish style. Turner's painting The Battle of Trafalgar was meant to become part of this commemoration.

'Now look at this so-called painting which your Turner, my lord, has concocted,' the King remarked, using words that provoked his first minister.

'With all respect, Majesty, I wish he was my Turner, but he is not, and if your Majesty allows, I also would not call this work a so-called painting.'

'So you wouldn't, would you?' asked the King, apparently indignant. On one hand he did not like being contradicted, but on the other hand he often intentionally provoked the opposition because he enjoyed the anger that resulted, which, because he was the King, they were unable to return.

'No, I wouldn't,' Liverpool responded. 'First of all, may I draw Your Majesty's attention to the care the painter took with this royal commission, his only one up to now, I venture to add. He did not hesitate to ask the admiralty for a plan of the flagship 'Victoria', thoroughly studied the technical details and acquired an astonishingly far-reaching knowledge of the navy in general. Deviating from his usual approach he even made two large preparatory sketches in oil. Thus he proved, not for the first time, his skill in accurately depicting ships.'

'This may be so,' said the King, 'but don't you recognize that Turner uses what you call his skill to create battle paintings in a way different from tradition? His intention, what most viewers do not seem to see, is, by means of ironic juxtapositions, to diminish the heroism of the battle and to bring the battle victims into the picture. Compare the picture with Philippe-Jacques de Loutherbourg's Lord Howe's Victory, or the Glorious First of June 1794 and you will see what I mean. You'll find it over there. The idea was to supplement that with Turner's painting.'

The King was now completely engaged. In spite of all his capriciousness, his obstinacy and political ignorance, his loose life, his drinking and unroyal behavior he was a man of taste, an art expert who could speak several foreign languages, among them German, French and Italian.

Gainsborough was one of his preferred painters. He loved the elegance and the subtle technique of Gainsborough's pictures and valued nothing more than The Morning Walk of 1785, done shortly before the marriage of the young couple portrayed. In this work the King found a dignity and grace expressed through a perfect harmony of landscape and figures reaching far beyond the usual portrait art.

Liverpool knew the King's preference and therefore responded cautiously:

'Your Majesty is an outstanding expert on art, and there is little that escapes Your Majesty. I believe that Turner tried to complement Loutherbourg's picture, though also to surpass it, as artists do, by concentrating on 'Victory', instead of depicting two hostile battling flagships. Please, Your Majesty, regard the drama represented. To the right of 'Victory' lies the badly damaged French 'Redoubtable', from which Nelson was shot and killed. The English flag flies over the French as a sign that the enemy ship was taken. Beyond the 'Victory' the Spanish flagship 'Santissima Trinidad' is just visible and behind it the stern of the French flagship 'Bucentaure'. To the left in the background the French 'Achille' is burning, and in the middle ground the English 'Temeraire' comes into view. Turner is concentrating on the moment when the 'Redoubtable' is taken, its crew has just surrendered as can be seen by their raised arms.'

'Quite right,' the King interjected, 'the painter is concentrating our and his attention on the moment. And that is exactly what I and others hold against him. He does not give the viewer a proper report of the battle which would have been fitting for such a great national event. What does he do instead? You tell me, my lord.'

The prime minister hesitated. Should he still try to persuade the King to keep the picture for its proposed purpose in the Royal Gallery, he would have to temporize and suppress what he really thought. But it seemed to him that the King had already made up his mind, and would probably not leave the painting here, in the St. James's Palace. Therefore, he decided to speak his mind freely.

'I think, Your Majesty, that Turner has painted his interpretation of the battle, not even intending to give an exact, objective account. And that, I find, is the right objective of the art of painting.'

'But dear lord, please consider the interpretation that Turner forces on us. And he does so using a great national event, which should raise the hearts and spur the viewers on to new heroic deeds. Do you see the dead and dying sailors? Do you see, or don't you, the French mariners on the 'Redoubtable', who desperately cling to the ship or are already dead?'

CHAPTER 16

The King went to the fireplace, in which a warming fire was burning, and grasped the bell pull that hung down beside it.

'Our talk will still take some time, my lord. Allow me to offer you some wine. I know that you would not accept my brandy.'

Without waiting for an answer, he pulled the cord, and when the valet entered, he instructed him to bring a bottle of claret and a glass. A glance at the decanter nearby informed him that he still had a consoling amount of brandy.

'Your Majesty is very gracious. I thank you for the offer of wine and also', Liverpool added in an attempt to gain an advantage, 'for allowing me to say freely what I think about the painting.'

After enjoying another draught of brandy, the King appeared calmer and more focused than at the beginning of the talk, and replied:

'You know, my lord, that I don't just want to make a decision about the picture.' He spoke in well-chosen words, expressing real interest. Contrary to the general public's view of his reputation, which admittedly he had acquired as Prince of Wales, George IV was a man of convictions and principles, which, though mainly restricted to his own person and the position of the crown, did not exclude compassion and humanness.

'Don't think that I am not sorry for the men who miserably died in the battle. But that is not the point here. Public spirit urgently needs the glorious representation of the great victories so that in future they too will be inspired to such deeds. But what does the painter do here? Look.'

He approached the painting and almost hit it with his forefinger.

'Here at eye level the viewer is forced to see the details of suffering and death. Don't you think this will distress them? That is at the core of Turner's interpretation rather than the glorious victory. The sea has a dirty brown color and one can see the trails of blood from the wounded seamen. This, I admit, is an unavoidable part of a victorious battle. But we have commissioned the painting to lift the spirit of the nation and not to arouse pity.

And here, you see, the painter is virtually prompting the viewers to be afraid of the secrets of the bottomless sea by showing a big part of the rigging as if it were a sea monster. And there, the man is looking at us with deathly fear in his eyes.

The hopelessness, suffering and death of unknown sailors represented side by side with famous admirals—believe me I have viewed the painting long enough—is not a confident invitation to new deeds for crown and empire.'

Liverpool stood before the picture and reflected. He could not but admire the surprisingly astute analysis of the King. Would God he could be of the same intellectual height in questions of politics and public affairs. With regard to the picture, the King was right from his point of view, and had more or less judged the artist correctly. And that, Liverpool thought, was proper. Everyone was allowed their own opinion about a piece of art. But the point here was that the King's view could have far-reaching consequences both for the artist and generally for the predominant forms of art.

He could no longer be silent without violating court etiquette.

'Your Majesty is right. Even in the moment of victory warning and remembrance are clearly expressed. But since Turner summarizes in one scenic allusion the events of the battle which were distributed over an extended period of time it does not give one a clear chronological understanding. Yes, for the purposes that Your Majesty intended the painting, it is probably not adequate. But may I remark that it is a great piece of art, which deserves appreciation?'

The King, quite at ease now, smiled and was, as seldom happened, content with the minister's answer.

'Your words about the greatness of the work I will not comment on. But to show you how I appreciate art and artists, I tell you that I have bought the painting and intend to present it to Greenwich Hospital together with Loutherbourg's works.'

With this he poured himself yet another glass of brandy and requested Liverpool to drink from the wine the valet had brought as a sign of the importance of this decision and the generosity he, the King, had shown.

PART 5
PILLNITZ NEAR DRESDEN, SEPTEMBER 1827

CHAPTER 17

There had not been a late summer like that in recent years. An unending blue sky spanned the earth and the sunny days never seemed to end. The branches of the apple trees were heavy with fruit, and on the heights above the Elbe the grapes were ripening, having had their full measure of sunshine.

All over the country people hoped for a good harvest and saw a connection between the blessings of the season and the accession to the throne of the new King, Anthony, full name Anton Clemens Theodor Maria Joseph Johann Evangelista Johann Nepomuk Franz Xavier Aloys Januar. New he was only as King, otherwise rather elderly, 72 in fact, now burdened with the difficult affairs of state.

King Frederick Augustus I had died without male offspring, so that now his brother came to inherit the throne. Generally, the Saxons were quite content with this, though not much was known about the new King. The main desire of the people was stability and clear agreement over the succession. It was rumored that Anthony was deeply religious and had said prayers of thanks for the emancipation of the Catholics by Napoleon. What the new King's nephew, thirty-year-old Prince Frederick Augustus, son of Anthony's younger brother Maximilian, who should originally have become King, wrote in his diary, did not become known: 'Anthony, having no idea of government, has reached an age of over 70 years without ever having taken part in any way in administration, organization and office, knows neither judicial systems nor state administration, has no insight into human nature and had been so little engaged in affairs of the state that he, without too sharp an intellect, will have no clear understanding of how to rule the kingdom. It is therefore quite natural that the decisions of the government, formerly taken by the King, are now in the hands of others. The real regent will be cabinet minister Count Einsiedel.'

Unaffected by such thoughts about the person of their new ruler, the professors of medicine Carl Gustav Carus, Heinrich Leopold Francke and Friedrich Ludwig Kreysig, the latter with wife, were on their way from Dresden to Pillnitz, traveling in a royal coach. The day was the 22nd of September, 1827. The small party enjoyed the fine weather and the changing scenery along the Elbe. They pointed out to each other the various ships that were to be seen on the river. Carus told them about a steamship he had seen ten years ago on the river Spree in Berlin. But here they did not encounter one. Their talk was more or less casual, as Carus and his colleague Francke were concentrating on the forthcoming audience with the King and his family, at which Kreysig would introduce Carus and Francke to the King as his new personal physicians.

When word had reached Carus of his appointment, he had at first not wished to believe it—with some reason. He would have to give up his official residence in the maternity clinic at the teaching institution for medicine and surgery, which he occupied as its director and professor of obstetrics. And the move, as he feared, would be accompanied by the usual troubles and unrest.

But to his and his wife's satisfaction they had found a fine large flat on the second floor of a house at the corner Moritzstrasse/Landhausgasse, with the disadvantage, though, that the beautiful view of the Elbe scenery was lost. Also, he had heard so much about the strict etiquette at court and the other difficulties attending service as personal royal physician that he doubted he would be able to satisfy the King's demands given his own desires for independence and freedom of expression.

On the other hand, he had felt so much honored both personally and professionally that in the end he had accepted the royal offer. And finally, the new occupation meant that he no longer had to undertake the troublesome effort of lecturing daily to young women about the rudiments of midwifery. This had been a large part of his work for many years and had become rather tiring.

'Mr. Kreysig,' he said now, turning to his colleague, 'do you really believe I can justify the trust I am being shown by this appointment? I am not a courtier, after all.'

Kreysig, almost twenty years older than Carus, who like the latter took a middle position between empirical medicine and Schelling's theoretical approach, had suggested Carus as well as his nephew Francke as royal physicians.

He now reassured Carus:

'You will soon see that the stiff ceremonial etiquette of the previous court has already been considerably reduced and that the new King is a very accommodating master. You can trust that my long service as the doctor of Minister von Einsiedel has given me useful insights into court life. And besides,' he added in a low voice with regard to the coachman, 'such a position at court has its advantages. Consider Goethe, or Schinkel in Berlin, who have proved that the wise man, serving royalty, can achieve much good.'

Carus, who felt that Kreysig was anxious to encourage him, could not forget how Goethe, with whom he had a close relationship both personally and in the areas of science and the humanities, had quite frequently complained about the obligations entailed by his office. And poor Schinkel in Berlin did not expressly complain but had been made ill by the excessive amount of work he was burdened with—either through a sense of responsibility or personal ambition, Carus was not quite sure. However, Carus was somewhat reassured by the time they stopped at the gondola, went aboard and were taken over the river by six oarsmen clad in yellow and blue fisherman's livery.

There, they climbed the large old Venetian-styled steps leading to the Riverside Palace that served King Anthony and his brother Max, also quite old, as a summer residence.

The professors, in view of the forthcoming royal audience, were dressed with the brown court frock with gold-spun buttons, silk stockings and buckled shoes. Count Vitzthum, Privy Councilor and minister, led the visitors to the room of the personal physicians of the King, beautifully appointed with elegant furniture, then introducing them to the royal family.

As Kreysig had indicated, the new King was direct, humorous and cordial, and with regard to their duties as personal physicians he said to Carus and Francke, 'If you check a few times a week that I am still alive, it is enough. Probably something quite different will require all your attention. You have been told that as Privy and Medical Councilors you will become members of the government, which is not without importance, because it is there that decisions are taken that concern the medical affairs of the state.'

After about half an hour, audience and introduction ended, and Vitzthum saw the visitors to the antechamber, when suddenly the King called:

'Professor Carus, could you spare me some time to go for a walk through the garden?'

And before Carus could answer, the King had taken him by the arm and quite unceremoniously led him out of the palace to the Japanese camellia, which had been standing in the English Garden after a long journey via Kew Gardens in London for forty years. The King sat on a bench and invited Carus to sit beside him. The physician was surprised how casually the King treated his concerns. He had heard that as still heir apparent he liked to walk alone to his garden outside the Pirna Gate and spend time there relaxing. Now as King he retained this habit, though watched by a guard who trailed some distance behind.

'I have asked you out here, Professor, because I would like to talk about some matters of art, above all painting, and here again about a certain painter with whom, I learned, you are well acquainted and even considered good friends.'

With these words he drew a sheet of paper, a letter it appeared, from the pocket of his overcoat and handed it to Carus.

'First, please read this application that Friedrich, in 1816, see here the date, the 10th of June 1816, wrote to the King, my brother. And then tell me if or rather what conclusions can be drawn with regard to Friedrich's political and social convictions.'

Reading over the long-winded address, Carus thought that the King must be rather naïve if he thought that he would voice something adverse concerning his friend. Or His Majesty had already formed an opinion and wanted in this indirect way to assess his new doctor. If so, he was cleverer than Carus had at first imagined.

He read: 'I was born in Greifswald in the former Swedish part of Pomerania and am now in the 42nd year of my life. Through my own inclination I started on the study of landscape painting. My first lessons I received in my hometown, later I attended the Royal Academy in Copenhagen. After having spent some time in Berlin and having occupied myself with this school of art I came to Dresden, now eighteen years ago, in order to continue my artistic work amidst the splendid treasures of art and surrounded by beautiful nature. So, in due course, I have spent a considerable part of my life under the paternal protection of Your Majesty, where the sciences and arts blossom, in a city that is rightly called the German Florence, and also among an honest population distinguishing themselves by their religiosity as well as their taste for art. Thus, Saxony has become my second fatherland and its inhabitants, my beloved countrymen, to whom I have loved to return every time I have been abroad. All this has reinforced my desire to conclude my life under Your Majesty's mild scepter, because I regard it as an honor and great fortune to be allowed to count myself among Your Majesty's most obedient subjects.

As I now, during my stay here, have had several gratifying opportunities to show my works at the yearly public exhibitions, not without the acclaim of the experts and art enthusiasts, and as I have been lucky enough to be able to advise young people in their endeavors to study the art of painting, I dare to place the request before Your Royal Majesty in all obedience, not forgetting that the Art Academy regrettably lost several of its members by death: that Your Royal Majesty will most graciously deign to grant me membership of the Dresden Academy of Arts and also allow me the salary that is part of this appointment. I most submissively beg Your Majesty to most graciously give the relevant orders ...'

Now look at that, Carus thought after having read the refined and supplicatory end of the letter, look how courtly my otherwise so gnarled friend can be in language and attitude, if it is required. And he is obviously not put off by a King who had been such a close ally of the hated French. Though, to be fair, he did not do more in the way of submission than was usual.

CHAPTER 18

Carus was surprised by the interest of the King in Friedrich and in painting. So far he had heard only that he liked composing music, and, though he was not really gregarious, had organized weekly musical evenings with some musicians, which were said to be rather unconventional. These rehearsals were usually concluded with a supper that was opened by the King with the words: 'We have worked, now let us eat.'

Carl Maria von Weber thought the crown prince's cantata Trionfo d'Imeneo, when he heard it in 1819, 'full of talent'.

For King Anthony music was an expression of religiosity and was best used for praising God. Life and art in general were looked upon by him sub specie aeternitatis, and he assessed all events and productions with this perspective.

Originally, he had been destined, as the second-born, to become a prior or bishop, and he had been quite content with this idea. But the King, his brother Friedrich Augustus, had worried about the succession because after twelve years his marriage had still been childless. So, at the urging of his brother, AD 1781 he had married the seventeen-year-old Charlotte, daughter of King Victor Amadeus III of Sardinia. She died of smallpox one year after the marriage, and Anthony believed this to be God's sign to refrain from taking a new wife too soon

Carus thought how being a king did not always mean a life of fulfillment. He remembered Schiller's words from Mary Stuart, Queen of Scots:

'Kings are only slaves of their estate,

Follow their own hearts they may not.'

Anthony, due to the early death of his wife, had no progeny either, but in the meantime, Friedrich August had fathered a girl which meant that he could hope for a son, too. Unfortunately, this hope was not fulfilled, whereupon the King insisted his brother marry again, since he had written in his testament, that Anthony, or his son should inherit the throne.

Anthony, as many of his princely peers, had to serve dynastic interests for the sake of the country's stability, and in 1787 married Maria Theresa, daughter of Emperor Leopold II. With her an emperor's daughter was again, after Maria Josepha, allied with the country, which mightily strengthened the self-esteem of the Saxons after the defeat in the Seven-Years-War. Also, she was wealthy, so that one could hope possible extravagances of the King would not unduly burden the country's treasury.

When she arrived in Dresden, the press reported that 'the wardrobe of the Serene Royal Bride of Prince Anthony had punctually arrived in 28 trunks. An exquisite, highly artful silver toilette, golden tableware and precious laces adorning all dresses likewise attracted the attention of the connoisseurs.'

What was even better, the bride brought half a hundredweight of ducats, exactly 111111, which the

Dresdeners were quick to translate into half a million guldens. A clever mind even calculated that you could buy 16,000 horses for the money. And added that a mason who earned 200 guldens per year would have to work about 2500 years to reach the bride's dowry. The court treasury paid an interest of 20,000 thalers annually on Maria Theresa's dowry, so that Anthony found himself richer than any other prince of the blood. Everybody expressed their satisfaction and was quite ready to ignore the fact that the bride had only one eye.

While Carus was pondering all this, the King sat beside him buried in thought, hesitating to begin the announced talk.

Carus remembered the fate of Charlotte, the King's first wife. She had died of smallpox before the beneficial discovery of cowpox inoculation by Edward Jenner came into widespread use in Europe. Having read Jenner's famous 'Inquiry into the causes and effects of the variolae vaccinae a disease … known by the name of the cow-pox' from 1798 Carus thought how good it was that medicine was now more and more based on empirical research and was no longer a simple repetition of the teachings of the classics.

Before he could continue thinking about how easily medical findings pass some people by and how it is therefore the duty of the doctor to constantly stay abreast with the latest knowledge, in a sense to separate the chaff of mere speculation from the wheat of proven discovery, the King began:

'Let me tell you how I came to be interested in Friedrich. Last year I visited the Prince of Prussia, the Crown Prince, in Berlin. Time has come, I believe, to get over the old antagonism between our countries. I admit this will not be easy for us, because we are still hurting from the loss of such a large part of our land.

The Crown Prince, 31 years of age, proved very understanding and was interested in everything connected with art and above all in painting. Also, he seemed inclined once he became king to contribute to the reconciliation of our two kingdoms.

He quite frequently mentioned his father's architect Karl Friedrich Schinkel, praised him highly and conceded that he owed his own proficiency in painting to Schinkel, who was not only a great master builder but also an excellent painter. His painting Castle by the River the prince said, was one of his favorite pieces. He liked it so much that he asked Consul Wagener, who had commissioned the painting, to bring it to his residence so that we were able to view it thoroughly. Do you, dear Carus, know this work?'

'I do, Majesty. When I was in Berlin two years ago, I had the chance to see the picture as well as the beginning of Schinkel's new museum building. The master himself showed me the drawings for the frescos he intended for the museum and explained them to me. The whole terrestrial and human world, as he called it, had provided him with ideas for the tablets, and I was deeply impressed by their fine water color technique and their intellectually stimulating and poetical content. His Majesty the King of Prussia can count himself fortunate to have such an architect and at the same time an excellent painting teacher for his son the Crown Prince.'

'That, too, had become clear to me in Berlin,' the King added. 'And I have plans for Schinkel here in Dresden, about which I ask you not to speak for the moment. As a kind of counterpoint to our Dresden baroque style I want Schinkel to design a guardhouse on the Theater Place, more slender than his Guardhouse in Berlin, which by the juxtaposition of baroque and classicism will certainly add to the attractiveness of the place.'

Carus nodded. 'Schinkel will doubtlessly like to carry out such a design and will also feel honored by Your Majesty's commission. I know that he does not like the baroque style very much, all the more will he be willing to design the counterpoint desired by Your Majesty, inspired by Greek antiquity.'

'I think so, too,' said the King. 'But now back to Schinkel's Castle by the River. How did you like it when you were in Berlin?'

'The painting,' Carus answered, 'seems to me to be a symbol of an old vanishing world. For the last resident of the castle, the old head forester, there is no place left for a grave. His body is taken over the river in a boat in order to be interred on the other side, which is painted as a world of hope and renewal under the sign of the cross.'

'Good that you stress the Christian character of the painting, Professor Carus. Because there are other things to be remarked, I think, namely an anti-French intention. The composition as a whole makes one think of Heidelberg Castle, which, destroyed by French troops in the War of the League of Augsburg, remained a ruin. You know that I don't at all like anti-French resentments, not forgetting that our ducal and royal house had been closely allied to Napoleon most of the time. By the way, Carus, were you not also kind of allied to the French so that you were to be awarded the Order of the Legion of Honor?'

'This medal, which by the way I have not received yet, is to be regarded exclusively in honor of my services as a physician, and I do not attach any—how shall I say—political importance to it.' Saying this Carus made a conciliatory gesture to take a certain sharpness out of his answer.

But the King did not seem to have noticed. He beckoned to a page waiting at the crossing of two parkways some distance away and ordered him to bring cold meat from the kitchen and a bottle of claret from the cellar.

'I hope you can spare me some more time, dear doctor. It is long after midday and you certainly won't refuse a glass of wine and some roast venison.'

Carus bowed his head and accepted the offer gratefully. Then he said:

'What I meant with regard to Schinkel's picture about the vanishing old world is the old feudal world of the knights and not at all the world of absolute princely rule and its inherent justice.'

The King, as Carus had hoped, showed himself very satisfied with this remark.

In the meantime, the page approached with one of the cooks. Obviously, they had been expecting that the King would offer his guest something to eat. They put a folding table in front of the gentlemen, covered it with a white cloth and added plates of fine translucent Meissen porcelain as well as glasses. Another kitchen staff brought the opened bottle of wine and cold meat on a plate. He said, as the cook had instructed him:

'Your Majesty, these cold meat slices are from leg of venison Italian style, which we had yesterday. We are hoping most humbly that Your Majesty will still enjoy it today.'

The King thanked the kitchen team and poured his guest and himself the wine, before Carus could do it.

'I hope such a diet, taken in moderation, is in compliance with your doctoral concepts.'

'Quite, Your Majesty,' said Carus, who liked a good bite himself. They drank their health, served themselves with the meat, which they ate with white bread.

While enjoying the meal, Carus reflected on his remark about absolute monarchy. Was that his true opinion or a concession to the tone usual at courts, with which he sought the good will of the King? Though was not his remark correct, per se? Under the absolute rule of a prince all subjects were equally dependent on his will, at least in theory. And all were equal under the King, of course not among themselves. But still he began to be upset with himself. Did he not wish to avoid becoming the usual obliging courtier?

After finishing some bread and meat and wiping his mouth with a fine white cloth, the King said:

'A short while ago I mentioned what had happened in Berlin. Now I am coming to my main concern. The Prince of Prussia showed me two paintings by our Dresden painter Caspar David Friedrich, Monk by the Sea and The Abbey in the Oak Wood. He told me his father, the King, bought them for him when he was just fifteen years of age. Now, Dr. Carus, I would like to hear what you think of the pictures, if you know them at all.'

'I do, Majesty. I even have two faithful copies at home, which a good friend of Friedrich's, Christian August Silberschlag, made. On the occasion of the successful birth of his first son, during which I could help his wife as her obstetrician, he gave them to me as a sign of gratitude. These two works—I am now speaking of the originals—were belatedly handed in for the 1810 Academy Exhibition in Berlin by the painter, where the King bought them, as I said before, at his son's insistence. At that time, I was a studiosus medicinae at Leipzig university and was preparing for my doctor's examination. This was to give me the chance to try my hand at academic teaching. It was a century-old tradition at the university to try for the title of a doctor philosophiae because it was the easiest to acquire for a young scholar. The basis for my application was my treatment ...'

Here Carus noticed the King's somewhat impatient gesture and realized he had become a little too detailed and should rather more directly answer the question. He recognized that at still a relatively young age of 38, he was becoming perhaps too inclined to these extended discursions.

'I beg Your Majesty's pardon for my digression,' he said. 'Friedrich made the two paintings as companions, belonging together, though seeming so different in design and content.'

'Now you have made me really curious,' remarked the King, 'how you will explain to me that the paintings belong together, admitting they are formally so different.'

He took his glass, drank Carus's health, which the latter responded to. The doctor then said:

'Your Majesty will allow me to give a little bit more detail on that. Monk by the Sea was first mentioned by Christian August Semler in an article in the *Journal des Luxus und der Moden* on a visit to Friedrich's studio in 1809. There Semler described the painting, which the artist must have begun soon after finishing the Tetschen Altar, also called Cross in the Mountains in 1808. It could have been earlier, though.'

'Surprising, what you are saying about the time of the creation of the picture. My impression is that it is a work of— how shall I say—sad serenity, even pessimism, that is to say rather a late work of the painter.'

'Yes, if one considers how unconventionally Friedrich goes about composing the image, using a quite new idea of perspective—it is undoubtedly astonishing.'

Here the doctor, without waiting for invitation from the King, refilled his own wine glass.

CHAPTER 19

In the meantime, the sun had wandered on, and the camellia cast a long shadow. But the mild September day still persisted, warming the King's rheumatic royal limbs very pleasantly, as he informed Carus.

'Yes, Your Majesty, warmth is good for this kind of limb pain. And I may for the affected limb recommend the application of Semen Sinapis nigrae or mustard poultice, tincture of iodine as well as rubbing in of spirituous and stimulating substances, for example spirit of camphor and volatile liniment. And please do not expose the royal body to cold draught as it is particularly to be expected in the fall. I will take the liberty to put my recommendations on paper tonight and send them to Your Majesty tomorrow morning. Please be gracious enough to send me your valet for this.'

'Do so, dear doctor, but I can't promise that I will follow all your recommendations. But I'll do my best.'

The King beckoned the page waiting nearby and ordered him to clear away the plates and then turned to Carus again.

'And now please give me your explicit opinion on the Monk,' the King said with a directness that did not leave room for maneuvering.

'What is unusual and admirable about this painting, Majesty, lies in the tension-filled void, contradictory as this may sound. The viewer as well as the monk find themselves confronted by boundless space. The small strip of sand borders sharply on the sea, whose surface in the picture is as large as the strand. However, it feels like a wider space. This seeming paradox indicates the metaphysical in the painting, defying understanding ...'

'Hold on a minute,' interrupted the King. 'Does that mean that the decisive effect of the background is not its size but its immeasurable quality? Did you mean that when you mentioned the metaphysical in the painting?'

'Absolutely, Your Majesty, that is what I meant. With no way to orient himself, the monk, in fact Friedrich himself, confronted with this vastness, realizes how small and helpless he is.

The third and greatest element is the sky. It is shown as the struggle of light over darkness, and as I know my friend Friedrich's religious convictions, it is the struggle to gain the divine promise of salvation and life eternal. The night sky with the morning star and the crescent of the waning moon which can only be seen in the early morning, express something similar, namely the promise of the coming daylight, which will triumph over darkness.'

'Your friend, dear Carus, if I can believe your words, seems to me to be a painter of symbols which he thinks he can find in the nature created by God. I like that, though this raising of nature to a religion does not quite correspond with my own faith.'

'Your Majesty is quite right here,' said Carus. 'And the monk is brooding, supporting his head in his hand, the classic gesture of mourning. He is brooding over the metaphysical that he senses in the landscape. And that is exactly what

Friedrich is doing as a painter, when he interprets landscape as symbolic. It is therefore completely justified that he himself is represented in the monk. He shows how he is exclusively oriented toward eternity and at the same time how lonely he is.'

Carus fell silent to allow the King a chance to respond, which he used immediately.

'All this sounds less political than I was told in connection with Friedrich and which made my late brother restrict as far as possible the painter's influence on young people with regard to academic teaching.'

'No, this painting is certainly not political in the sense we understand it today. And I believe, Your Majesty, that Friedrich is firstly a religious and only secondly a political painter. By the way, what I said about the monk's loneliness as portrayed in the painting gives me some reason to be worried. I hope that Friedrich will have the strength to escape from his depressive tendencies as they are visible here and also in the counterpart, Abbey in the Oak Wood. Because there is no doubt that despite all belief in salvation and forgiveness the paintings impart a distinct impression of deep sadness and homelessness, which gives rise to concern about the painter's mental state.'

'Well, yes, let's talk about the Abbey. Here my first impression was one of ice-cold death.'

'That wouldn't do the painting justice because it does not take into regard the waxing moon and the bright evening sky as symbols of life eternal. Besides, I may say that good as I find Monk by the Sea, I prefer The Abbey in the Oakwood.

May I cite to you a sonnet by Theodor Körner, who as far as I can judge, understood the meaning of the painting correctly, just as Friedrich wants it to be understood?'

'Hold on,' the King almost shouted, 'Körner, you are saying? Was he not the unfortunate person who had joined the insurgent Lützow and fought the emperor in his back and against the rules of the law of war? I am not quite sure, but had not already Hugo Grotius in his famous work De jure belli ac pacis or On the Law of War and Peace declared this kind of warfare unjust? I for one utterly condemn it.'

Carus, who was troubled by the King's vehemence, said gently:

'I implore Your Majesty not to get too excited and spoil this fine afternoon for Your Majesty. Besides, such an agitation does the royal blood no good. It may start rushing, even foaming and imbalance the healthy humors. Majesty will certainly look at Körner and the sonnet mentioned with more gracious eyes if you remember his father, who performed honorably when serving Dresden as Russian government counselor. Christian Gottfried Körner was a friend of Schiller's and gave shelter to the poet several times in his Dresden home and on his vineyard at Loschwitz. When I was a boy I was once lucky to meet the famous poet on the property of the Göschen family in Hohenstädt near Grimma. I remember him as a tall, respectable man in a blue overcoat who was pointed out to me when we children were absorbed in playing so that my memory is only a fleeting one.'

It was Carus's intention to speak at length in order to give the King time to compose himself so that he would be able to calmly listen to Körner's poem Friedrich's Scenery of Death.

He thought the King might now be ready to listen but as soon as he had started with 'The earth lies silent in deep deep mourning', the King interrupted him.

'No, Carus, don't go on. I don't know how you can believe I would like to hear the production of this rebellious subject.'

Carus was not greatly disturbed by this response since he already considered himself the King's physician and could view his patient with some indulgence. After a short pause he said:

'Allow me now, Your Majesty, to speak about the connection of the two paintings. Friedrich once said: "The artist should paint not only what he sees before him, but also what he sees within him. If, however, he sees nothing within him, then he should also refrain from painting that which he sees before him. Otherwise, his pictures will be like those folding screens behind which one expects to find only the sick or the dead."

This is how Friedrich understood the profession of the painter or rather the artist in general. Meditation about death as transition and salvation seems to me to be the most important leitmotif of Monk by the Sea. This meditation leads one to its counterpart, The Abbey in the Oakwood, which by its aura of solemnity has a calming effect despite the bizarre shapes of the naked oaks.

The procession of the coffin-bearing monks moves through the gate of the church ruin past the open grave toward the crucifix and the haze-filled background, symbolizing that not the grave but eternity is the goal of earthly life.

There is a—how shall I say—variant or other version of the Abbey, which is called Monastery Graveyard in the Snow. This I find less to my taste since here architecture plays too distinct a role as it sometimes does in Friedrich's paintings. This impairs, I think, the freedom of the landscape, and the symbolism no longer emanates from it naturally but seems to be impressed on it from outside. But not so in the Abbey.'

'You have expressed this beautifully and plausibly, Carus,' the King said. 'Yes, the two paintings belong together, and now I recognize the funeral procession of the Abbey is the procession of the monk, or Friedrich himself, from Monk by the Sea.'

'And there is more to it,' said Carus. 'If one considers that the model for the Abbey, the ruins of the Cistercian monastery of Eldena, lies on the Baltic, then, unusual as it may sound, Monk and Abbey are two sides of one coin. And, Your Majesty, I know Friedrich well enough to say that such hints, which may not be evident to the untutored viewer, are indications of Friedrich's manner of communicating personal thoughts and aspirations in a cryptic way. For example, that the world for him is a valley of tears is an article of faith, and is as certain as media vita in morte sumus.'

'Yes,' the King agreed, 'in the midst of life we are in death.'

'May I ask Your Majesty to graciously listen to the following verses by Friedrich:

Oft have I been queried why
I paint of death, the grave, the transitory?
The answer is that all must die
To live in all eternity.

'But how, dear Carus, do the wild and bizarre, almost ghostly oaks, which no doubt are symbols of Germanic paganism, fit into Friedrich's Christian image?'

'It is the contrast, Majesty, which the painter symbolically makes use of here. The eerie unrest of the oaks is set against the measured rhythm of the funeral procession. The crescent moon stands for Christ as the light illuminating the night of death. The full moon can already be divined, though not seen clearly, as the promise of a brighter future.

And the Gothic ruin stands in one row with the oaks, the symbols of paganism and so also indicates the bygone medieval piety. Now here Your Majesty will certainly think otherwise, but for Friedrich the unfathomability of nature takes on the function that the church traditionally had.'

'Of course, I differ here. Church is church and nature is nature, and to mix the two of them up and believe that looking at nature can replace worship service does not seem right to me and is against the teachings of the Catholic, the only true church, which holds that extra ecclesiam nulla salus.'

'Friedrich's artistic opinions can be best understood if they are compared with those of other painters, for example the Norwegian Johann Christian Clausen Dahl, who came to Dresden in 1818 and moved in with Friedrich in '23. The two are friends and I feel honored to be part of this friendship.

There is hardly a sharper contrast than the one between Friedrich and Dahl in how they look upon landscape. Dahl is a pure naturalist. He depicts the details of rocks and trees and herbs and meadows masterfully, paints with extraordinary skill, but lets pure chance sometimes play too big a role. He tends to lose himself as much in the objective detail as Friedrich loses himself in his subjective approach. Despite these differences Dahl is a simple and faithful soul with a kind heart and Friedrich's true friend. Friedrich cannot look at the world with the eyes of naturalists like Dahl or Goethe do, though he observes nature very closely. He once said to me that he is afraid of a kind of scientification of nature because then it would lose its soul. Therefore, he does not accept or even understand Goethe's approach, who does not look at nature as a mythical power surrounding man but tries to grasp it in its very essence, its innermost laws, more like a mathematical or physical problem to be solved. This approach, I confess, is mine, too.

May I ask if Your Majesty knows Dahl, who is said to be a renewer of Norwegian landscape painting?'

'How much I would like to say that at least I have heard of him. No, I haven't. But we will come to the problem of me not knowing such an artist later.'

Suddenly the King shivered. A cool evening breeze had come up and blew from the direction of the Elbe. Carus stood up quickly, bowed and said:

'I beg Your Majesty urgently to warm yourself in the palace. It has become quite chilly during our talk.'

'The most important matter I have on my mind I almost forgot. Your mention of a well-known painter with whom I am not familiar has reminded me. Our talk was meant firstly to clarify my opinion of Friedrich, whereby you have laudably helped me, even though I have not heard you saying a word about his letter to my late brother the former King. As you know Friedrich was appointed Associate Professor of our Royal Art Academy though without being entrusted with teaching the class of landscape painting. I think I can now imagine what caused my immortalized royal brother to slight the painter in this way. And I am not sure how I will decide, if it is even possible to change that decision. But we will have opportunities to talk this matter over again. Because now I come to my second reason for having you here. I wanted to ask you, besides your tasks as my personal physician, to help me in questions of the visual arts, should they arise. Here in Dresden it can often occur that the King has to comment on matters concerning art, and I would not like to appear too ignorant on such occasions.'

'I feel very honored by Your Majesty's request,' Carus replied.

The King hailed the page and ordered him to tell the equerry to get a coach ready to take Carus home, this time via the Pirna'sche Landstraße since the oarsmen had already been dismissed for the day.

PART 6
DRESDEN, SEPTEMBER 1835

CHAPTER 20

The weather was not at its best when the English painter Joseph Mallord William Turner arrived in Dresden on Saturday, September 19th, 1835, having taken the stagecoach from Meissen.

The journey from Berlin usually required just 24 hours, but Turner had stopped over in Wittenberg and Elsterwerda. He had long desired to visit the actual site of Martin Luther's activities in Wittenberg wanting to learn more about the reformer, who in his tract Martinus Lutherus contra Henricum Regem Angliae had written so scathingly about the 'Defender of Faith', King Harry. Turner did not forget, though, that Luther, after the King had broken with Rome in order to marry Anne Boleyn, felt compelled, with embarrassment, to change his view of the King and regard him more positively.

It was still raining when Turner arrived in Dresden as it had during the entire journey, and the view of the city was a disappointment to him, though he rebuked himself for this thought. Silberschlag had described Saxony quite differently, and his description had possibly been clouded by homesickness during his visit to London in the cold November weather—that was about twenty years ago, hard to believe how fast the years flew by.

Still, Turner harbored expectations. First of all, he hoped to find inspiration for sketches and pictures in this beautiful city and lovely surroundings with its rivers, castles, forests and architectural gems. Secondly, he was looking forward to meeting the Saxons, about whom Silberschlag had told him much. He had mentioned their friendliness toward foreigners, their generally good education and love of everything connected with art, and above all their interesting dialect with its soft consonants and its diphthongs and not quite proper use of grammar. Silberschlag, though not being a pure Saxon, had done his best to explain this language variant to Turner.

Thirdly, and this was most important to him, he would be seeing Silberschlag again, the good friend of his London days, with whom he had, during the interval, communicated only by letter. Through him, Turner hoped to meet the legendary Caspar David Friedrich and see the paintings he had heard much about. This painter was said to embody the true sense of everything German. Turner had traveled widely in Germany and though he had come to know the country's varied attractions, he felt the German character had remained elusive. Perhaps knowing Friedrich could help him. He could hardly wait.

How to describe what it means to be German? How does it differ from being English? Is it more truly expressed in this part of Germany, in the land of Luther and Bach? But Friedrich had come from the North of Germany, which at the time of his birth was Swedish, and Goethe was no Saxon but had come from the west, or rather south-west of the country. The English translation of his Theory of Colors had given Turner much to think about, especially the idea that Goethe was not concerned with the physical analysis or synthesis of colors but was aiming at their sensual and ethical effects. And he had detected a phenomenon that could be called subjective color. Though a complicated matter Turner hoped to be able to make use of it for his painting. He particularly liked the sentence in the Theory of Colors about the effects of color design, in which Goethe states that the totality of color appears to the eye as a single object and through it the sum of the work creates a separate reality. O yes, Turner thought, that is what painting really is about.

First of all, he would indulge in the luxury of seeing and sketching and not bother with problems of color theory and the German character, which are not easy to be solved anyway. And besides, it is possible that the character, the essential nature of a people can be best divined through its history and its landscape.

The special issue of the newspapers Dresdner Anzeiger of the following day would certainly announce his arrival in the Hôtel de Russie, conveniently situated in the Wilsdruffer Strasse, which ran in a western direction from the Altmarkt to the Wildsdruffer Platz and to the Zwinger palace. In Reichard's 'Manual du Voyageur en Allemagne' it stood at the top of the list of the Dresden hotels, and this had made Silberschlag recommend it to Turner, though for the following days he had offered Turner accommodation in his home.

The journey to Dresden had, on the whole, been rather troublesome, though Turner felt that next time, if there ever was a next time, it would be easier since the resourceful Saxons were planning to build a railway between Dresden and Leipzig, which it was said was already under construction.

The coachman unloaded the luggage in front of the hotel closely watched by Turner, who worried about his painting supplies. Only then did he take time to look around. The rain had stopped, and bits of a blue sky began to appear. And, quite unexpectedly at this moment, an older man called out to him in a cheery voice. At first the painter did not recognize him. How Silberschlag had changed! He was almost bald, wore round thick glasses, and under his frock coat a stomach bulged. But what he had not lost was his vivacity and the ability to approach a person openly, conveying to them his own good mood.

'You can't believe how happy I am to finally welcome you here in Dresden, Mr. Turner. It is hardly to be believed: Turner in Dresden. Look, even the sun has broken through in greeting.'

He grasped the hand of the painter and shook it vehemently. And indeed, the joy at seeing Turner again brought tears to his eyes.

Turner, who was uncomfortable with such emotional outbursts but did not want to hurt his friend's feelings, grasped Silberschlag's hand firmly, though a bit awkwardly, and said: 'Dear friend, you seem to be really excited. I feel much honored. And let me thank you for offering me accommodation in your home for a few days. This allows us to be near each other and saves me money at the same time. I call this killing two birds with one stone. I hope I won't be too much trouble for you and your dear wife.' He said this in

English, which made a Dresdener, standing nearby, ask the question, 'You're not from here, are you?'

Turner said, 'Nein', resorting to his sparse German, and turned back to Silberschlag, who strongly dismissed the possibility that Turner could inconvenience them in any way.

'Not at all, my honorable friend. Since my wife's parents passed on, we have room enough. And our two eldest have left home. Friedemann studies at the Forestry Academy in Tharandt, and Erdmute is married to a worthy pathologist in Halle on the Saale river, by the way the birthplace of your or rather our common composer Handel. They have three children, so you see that I am now a happy grandfather. And my two youngest, twins, as you know, who made it difficult for Dr. Carus at my wife's delivery, are still schoolchildren and quite well.'

So speaking, he took up Turner's valise and carried it toward the hotel entrance. The porter and his helper then assisted with the big trunk and the rest of the boxes.

Inside they awaited their guest, though he had not followed immediately. Going back outside, Silberschlag found him standing with a sketchbook and drawing with determined strokes the contours of the Frauenkirche, Church of Our Lady, which loomed over the roofs of the neighboring houses. The clouds had further dissipated and the mild September sun was shining. Turner snapped his sketchbook shut, said to Silberschlag he would continue with this sketch the next day and let himself be led into the hotel lobby, where he entered his name, nationality and home address into the large guestbook.

CHAPTER 21

Turner lay awake in the guestroom of Silberschlag's home. Though trying hard he could not find sleep. The bed blanket he felt hardly deserved this name, being really just a big linen tube or hose stuffed with goose feathers. And the idyllic evening in the Silberschlag family had made him especially thoughtful so that he was unable to find rest. He compared his own situation with that of his host, and it made him wonder if he had missed something in his life. The steady and permanent love of a woman, a wife, a consort for life?

That evening had been what the Germans so fittingly called gemütlich, a term that was difficult to translate. Perhaps cozy came nearest. Frau Johanna, whom Turner had only known through Silberschlag's loving tributes, had proved to be an excellent hostess. As they could not afford a maid, she had engaged a woman-helper for the evening and with her aid prepared a substantial meal. And then she had easily and unselfconsciously taken part in the vivid debate that ensued between her husband and their visitor from England. It turned out she was surprisingly well informed about many aspects of art, politics and social life, had a great wealth of ideas and was able to put her husband right on many a point, though in a very friendly and loving manner. Turner was surprised and began to think that perhaps a wife might be able to enrich his own life as well, perhaps even adding an additional dimension to his painting.

The supper, or dinner, as Turner would have called it, started with a green soup. To prepare this, cut one leak into fine stripes, sweat them lightly in 1 table-spoon of butter and put it aside. Sweat 2 table-spoons of wheat flour for a short time taking care that the flour does not brown. Bring it to boil in 2 liters of beef bouillon and by letting it simmer reduce it by 1/3. Keep the heat low and stir frequently. Pour the soup through a sieve and return it to a boil. Add a handful of chervil, sorrel and purslane and a small head of lettuce, season allowing, as well as the sweated leek. Take it from the fire and thicken with egg yolk mixed with a cup of cream.

Frau Silberschlag had seasoned the soup with salt and nutmeg and brought it to the table with two toasted slices of white bread.

The main dish was beef rolls, which she called rouladen, with dumplings partly made from raw potatoes. They were quite new to Turner. That potatoes were already available in September was due to the introduction of a medium-early variety, spreading throughout Saxony, which meant that this practical earth fruit was available most of the year. Farmers had learned to dig pits or clamps which preserved the potatoes over the winter.

'I take 10 medium-sized peeled raw potatoes,' Frau Johanna explained to her guest, who had asked for the recipe. 'I grate them into a bowl with a good amount of cold water, let them rest a while and then press them through a cloth. Then I boil another ten peeled potatoes and put them through a potato ricer. These I mix thoroughly with a cup of hot milk, a table-spoon of wheat flour and quickly combine them with the pressed, salted raw potato mass. I then wet my hands and form large round dumplings, in the middle of which I put bread crumbs fried in butter. The dumplings are then boiled or rather simmered in salted water. Now the ability of the cook is tested because she must find the right point of time at which the dumplings are ready. After all the dumplings have risen to the surface, I take one out and sample it. The inside must be dry and crisp. If you shake a dumpling the bread crumbs should be heard rattling inside it. You can see for yourself, Mr. Turner, if I have succeeded.' With these words Frau Johanna gave the visitor a sheet of paper with the recipe, which her husband had translated into English.

Even without the red cabbage, which according to custom should be eaten with this meal but due to the season was not available, everybody fell in heartily and praised Frau Johanna's efforts. Beer was served. The twins had already been sent to bed having been fed bread, milk and butter, for normally the Silberschlags did not have a warm meal in the evening.

After the meal they had sat together longer than they had in the first days of Turner's visit. Johanna's English proved to be so good that she could converse with their guest without much difficulty. It turned out that she had spent much time in acquiring this fine language. She had found it easy at the beginning, but diving deeper into its intricacies confessed that it was impossible to learn it even to half perfection.

Turner turned in his bed and tried to arrange himself so that he was enfolded on all sides, preventing the cool air from the open window getting at him. On the bedside table a nightlight was burning. At the foot of the bed stood a chair with Turner's clothes, and on which there was one of Silberschlag's nightcaps. Turner had not thought of using it. A chamber pot stood beside the chair.

Between the two windows was a chest of drawers, the drawers having curved fronts with decorative inlays. On the chest was a bunch of wild flowers that the children on their way home from school had gathered for their guest. There was also a water jug, a glass, two candles and between them a small clock. Above it on the wall hung a medium-sized oil painting, about 12 by 10 inches. In the wall opening under the other window stood a small square table and beside it a padded stool.

In the flickering candle light Turner could just make out these objects. He was in a strange mood. This room with its shiny scrubbed floor boards, so practical and modest, was like a small self-contained, warm and safe world which attracted him and at the same time made him feel uneasy, as if attempting to entice him to something he deeply resented, the allure of complacency. He had felt this in a vague sense since first setting foot in Silberschlag's house.

Their talks had strengthened this feeling. The Silberschlags hardly went out, preferred singing, playing the piano and reading books and journals to each other or their friends at home. And Silberschlag had started a great hymn to contentment and simplicity in which nature is not man's enemy but is there for his good because it is God's creation. When Turner came to talk about Silberschlag's journey through England it almost seemed as if the latter wanted to regard that chapter of his life as closed and not to be repeated, neither in words nor in practice.

The nightcap on the chair almost seemed to the painter a symbol of this new ethos which he thought he could recognize in his host. Modest self-restraint, taming of the passions, quiet submission to fate, an acceptance of a modest achievement, a prudent fortune, love of domestic detail, history and nature now replaced for Silberschlag what was previously a longing for new insights, the wish to discover life in all its grim and beautiful manifestations, desire for women and generally for nature, as well as a penchant for pointed arguments, for political dispute and change.

When Silberschlag explained his current attitude, Turner thought he could detect in the eyes of Frau Johanna a certain slight disdain. Perhaps he would find a chance for a talk with her privately, which would help him to understand Silberschlag's change of mind and what Johanna thought of it.

Considering this new attitude, it seemed almost a small miracle that Silberschlag had Friedrich's oil painting Snow-Covered Hut hanging on the wall when Turner arrived. Silberschlag had told him it was a copy, made by himself, of the painting Friedrich had shown at the Dresden Academy exhibition eight years before. It had been purchased on that occasion by Prince Johann Georg von Sachsen.

Silberschlag had not lost his good taste in pictures, as Turner remarked when he talked about the painting with him.

It was the first work or rather copy of a work by Friedrich that Turner had had the chance to see, and today like on the other days of his stay in Silberschlag's home he had stood before it for quite a long time when his host had left him alone in his room. He looked at it and tried to visualize for himself the painter, to discover what his inner feelings would have been when painting.

A modest subject, seen from quite near, is represented almost like a still life. A hut buried in hay lies under a thick cover of snow. The door is opened a bit and allows a glance into the darkness within the hut. The hay, so Silberschlag had explained, is according to the bible, man whose life elapses as stated in Psalm 37: 'For they shall soon be cut down, and wither as the green herb.' The haystack is his poor earthly dwelling, the darkness of which also hints at the grave.

Here Silberschlag had conceded that though he was well acquainted with Friedrich and his paintings these symbols were not immediately clear to him but had to be explained by the painter. The broken-down branches and the dried flowers symbolized life gone by. The representation of winter as a metaphor for dying, for death, would be quite frequent in Friedrich's works. But the symbols of passing away and death would always be connected with the remembrance of spring as a parable for resurrection. This idea, Silberschlag had said, would come to mind when viewing the dried-up flowers and the willow trees behind the haystack. Willow trees, which every year put out new shoots are also an indication of resurrection.

Turner, tossing and turning in his bed, thought this explanation did not make sense, at least seemed doubtful. A picture should not need elaborate explanations but should reveal itself on its own even to the untutored eye. If he had the chance to talk to Friedrich, and he hoped very much he would, he would try to discuss symbols in painting, the portrayal of reality and the impression created in the viewer. Because the Snow-Covered Hut could be interpreted quite simply, too, namely as a picture of longing for death and of final abandonment, as an icy and desperate picture of dying, underlined by the bleak gray sky in the background.

He threw the thick blanket off, got up, went to the chest of drawers and poured himself a glass of water. Then he took the few steps to the window and looked out. The moon was high in the sky and threw an eery light on the street, which lay deserted. The clock on the chest showed almost midnight. Truly it was calmer here than in London. Here, town and country had gone to sleep.

Tomorrow he would make further sketches of the city and ask Silberschlag to show him yet more interesting sights. And in some days, hopefully sooner than later, he could perhaps meet Friedrich and talk with him.

Helped by Silberschlag's expert guidance he had already seen much and made many sketches, foremost among them the one of the Frauenkirche, which he had begun on the day of his arrival.

The day after tomorrow they would start for the mountainous region called in German, he remembered, Sächsische Schweiz, which he translated into 'Saxon Switzerland'. There he was looking forward to the Bastei, a rock formation towering about 640 feet above the Elbe river. His sketchbook, begun in Copenhagen, was already full, and so, with his friend's help, he had acquired a new one that day. It was of blue woven paper of no great quality, but it would serve his purposes well. He could have made the purchase himself since while still in England he had compiled a little language guide with words and phrases for his German trip, phrases like 'Ich möchte nach Berlin fahren', (I would like to go to Berlin), 'Wie weit ist es bis ...', (How far is it to ...), 'Wo finde ich hier ein öffentliches Haus?', (Can you show me the way to a brothel?) as well as vital words like Gepäck for luggage, Geld for money, Zeug for stuff, things, clothes, kaufen for buy, verloren for lost.

The painter drank the water, put the glass back on the chest, used the chamber pot to relieve himself and went back to bed. He was able to quiet his thoughts and soon fell asleep.

CHAPTER 22

Friedrich woke up long before sunrise, looked through the window at the fading stars and then at his wife Caroline lying beside him. She was fast asleep, but restless, and from time to time her lips moved and she murmured incomprehensible words.

The painter rose noiselessly, tiptoed around the marital bed and bent over his wife. Perhaps he could make out what she was saying in her sleep and of whom she was dreaming. Then he could question her more intensely than he had been able to do the evening before. His suspicion that she went around with other men must be proved by hard evidence, if he wanted to end his being humiliated.

Though he did what he could to prevent it. He had restricted contact with friends like Silberschlag and Carus, whom he suspected she had an eye for.

Several times Carus had reprimanded him for his groundless jealousy and once even spoken directly to him about the almost pathological character it suggested. Carus believed, as he had told Friedrich in a quiet hour, that the cause of this jealousy might somehow be found in Friedrich's early attempt at suicide, which had fortunately not succeeded. This must have had, Carus said, a vague and dark after-effect on his disposition, which tended anyway to somberness. It had greatly affected his art and perhaps resulted in a permanent dissatisfaction with his own efforts. Friedrich should try to clearly understand this and bravely face it as an illness that could be cured. Carus made it quite plain to him: Only if Friedrich understood and accepted his diagnosis could he hope to rid himself of the brutal and frequent fits of temper toward his relatives and his wife and avoid the constantly growing isolation and loneliness that resulted.

Brutal fits of temper, really! Should he forget that she cheated on him? What was she murmuring now in her sleep? Was it a name? He could not understand her. He became dizzy and stood upright again.

For Carus, as a doctor, it was all very well to talk like this, Friedrich thought. And perhaps this was only meant to divert attention from himself. Had he not seen secret glances pass between his friend and Caroline when he visited the children, Agnes Adelheid and Gustav Adolf, both of whom had come down with measles?

He felt the pulse beating in his temples and his head seemed to swell with the rising blood. He was afraid of passing out completely as had already occurred several times. In such moments he could not remember what he had done or what had happened.

He stole out of the room, put on the old, long, gray and paint-stained travel coat and stopped before his easel with the oil painting The Sea of Ice, which he had subtitled The Wreck of Hope. He had put it there yesterday because he wished to examine it at leisure. There no longer appeared to be buyers of his work. The time when his name was talked about everywhere seemed now long over. But he did not intend to make concessions to the changing taste of the general public.

Instead, he would adhere to what he thought right and truthful.

This painting had been inspired by the panorama of Johann Carl Enslen, depicting a North Pole expedition in winter, which had been shown in 1822 to 1823 in Dresden and Prague. Additionally, he had read newspaper reports and seen visual representations of other polar expeditions. This was a topic that interested people. Ice drifts on the Elbe had helped him imagine broken ice floes.

But this was not the primary motive for his work, though people obviously wished to see representations of such adventurous trips.

Other aspects were more important. He was not interested so much in the sensational features of the polar world, but he had chosen the subject as a symbol of the inaccessible majesty of God. The eternal ice meant the eternity of God, meanwhile the shipwreck stood for the helplessness and transience of man and the futility of understanding God's essence by means of pure reason. Though the horrors of the polar world were not his main concern, the grandeur and solemnity of that world could not be overlooked in his representation. And the observer was meant to climb the ice floes like the steps of a temple to the level on which the icebergs reach for the blue clear sky. It was mistakenly said that the artist's intentions with the work had been political because the picture was intended to show the collapse of hopes for political change after the wars against Napoleon. But people's desire for pleasure had been so great that they overlooked his metaphysical approach. Even the good King of Prussia voiced bewilderment when the painting was shown in Berlin in 1826. He had said: 'The ice in the north certainly looks different', thus restricting the meaning of the picture to a mere superficial representation of polar ice. As if this was what the painter had aimed at.

People began to prefer the style of painting that was practiced in Düsseldorf– academic, genre painting with popular subjects and portraits. With them color and texture were suspect, and a focus on drawing and organized composition was stressed. How could he go along with that?

The roar in his head and the pulsing in his temples seemed to increase.

He left the room, passed by the nursery, went down the stairs, where he stepped into his shoes, and walked out. The fresh and cool night air helped reduce the pressure in his head for the moment.

He headed down to the Elbe and then along the left bank upstream toward Loschwitz.

On the right over the river hung a morning mist, in which indistinct figures were moving toward the bank. Were Erlking's daughters at large again? And who was whispering into his ear? He seemed to recognize Goethe's voice, deep, enticing yet threatening, Goethe, first his patron, then his adversary, who had said of his works that they should be smashed over the edge of a table.

Who rides there so late through the night dark and drear?
The father it is, with his infant so dear;
He holdeth the boy tightly clasp'd in his arm,

He holdeth him safely, he keepeth him warm.
'My son, wherefore seek'st thou thy face thus to hide?'
'Look, father, the Erl-King is close by our side!
Dost see not the Erl-King, with crown and with train?'
'My son, 'tis the mist rising over the plain.'
'Oh, come, thou dear infant! oh come thou with me!
For many a game I will play there with thee;
On my strand, lovely flowers their blossoms unfold,
My mother shall grace thee with garments of gold.'
'My father, my father, and dost thou not hear
The words that the Erl-King now breathes in mine ear?'
'Be calm, dearest child, 'tis thy fancy deceives;
'Tis the sad wind that sighs through the withering leaves.'
'Wilt go, then, dear infant, wilt go with me there?
My daughters shall tend thee with sisterly care;
My daughters by night their glad festival keep,
They'll dance thee, and rock thee, and sing thee to sleep.'
'My father, my father, and dost thou not see,
How the Erl-King his daughters has brought here for me?'
'My darling, my darling, I see it aright,
'Tis the aged grey willows deceiving thy sight.'
'I love thee, I'm charm'd by thy beauty, dear boy!
And if thou'rt unwilling, then force I'll employ.'
'My father, my father, he seizes me fast,
For sorely the Erl-King has hurt me at last.'
The father now gallops, with terror half wild,
He grasps in his arms the poor shuddering child;
He reaches his courtyard with toil and with dread,
The child in his arms finds he motionless, dead.

But it was not Erlking's daughters who appeared from the mist, but his long-dead brother Johann Christoffer. He came to his side and they walked together in silence. Friedrich marveled how tall the boy of his childhood had grown. Johann had drowned while skating with him in Greifswald and had wanted to save him after Friedrich had broken through the ice.

'What are you doing to your wife, Caspar?' asked Johann Christoffer, 'tormenting her without reason? And with this you torment yourself. You had already begun when you painted Woman at the Window.'

Friedrich was silent. His brother had drowned, now he was here. The blood began to roar and throb in his head, a bloody cloud passed before his eyes. He turned to Johann Christoffer.

'The woman sees the light of the unearthly, the heavenly Jerusalem beyond the river and the world. Her spirit escapes from the world, the dark inner room, in which her body remains imprisoned as long as she has to live. Her soul, her mind are freed and are carried across the water to the other world, like Charon, the ferryman, carries the souls of the newly deceased over the river. What do you want, Christoffer? The woman, my wife Caroline, in my art, is distinguished by love and hope. Though this was before she went astray.'

His brother walked by his side; his steps inaudible.

'Look into yourself, Caspar. The emptiness of the picture emanating from the broad floor boards, from the naked walls and the window soffits speaks otherwise. You have placed the woman in your studio, though everybody knows that you regard it as your own inviolable realm of work and meditation.'

'But in this way I have accorded her a place in my life and my work, and how does she thank me for it?'

Suddenly in front of them the crunching of wheels on the gravel path could be heard. Johann Christoffel disappeared when a junk dealer approached with his handcart, drawn by him and his dog. They passed without any sign of acknowledgment. Then again Friedrich heard Christoffer's voice: 'Listen, brother. You know, sometimes a painting happens within you, and despite careful planning, it brings to light what you perhaps did not intend. From that enclosed world in the painting, sober, grey, even bleak, the woman looks into the rich distance, to the river, to ships and trees.'

Friedrich tried to object. 'How can you know, brother, in your other world ...'

Johann Christoffer did not allow him to continue. 'Don't talk to me about the hereafter, which I should know better. In your painting Caroline is looking into the luminous blue of the sky, a representation of man longing for stability in the unstoppable flow of time. Your room is a prison from which the woman wants to escape, to be free, no longer bound to household, family, you—therefore your study, though ill-equipped for a life in freedom. And now, to top it all, you make her life difficult by your senseless, crazy, unfounded jealousy. I, not you, have reason to be jealous, jealous of life, your life, which should by rights be mine, because I have only lent it to you. I was almost saved, lying on the ice, when the young man, who was holding me, lost his meerschaumpipe and, trying to grab it, let go of me, I fell back into the water and was lost.'

His voice with his last words had become weaker and finally lost itself in the roar that Friedrich heard in his ears. His look became confused and he felt dizzy. In front of him a leaf detached itself from a tree and floated to the ground. When he tried to follow it with his eyes, darkness fell upon him. He felt painful guilt, constricting his chest and heart. Swaying he reached for a tree in support, but his hand missed and he fell to the ground.

CHAPTER 23

Palsy, apoplexia cerebri, is a sudden disturbance of brain activity due to the disruption of the circulation of the blood in a part of the brain. Most frequently this happens in the form of a stroke which shatters the brain matter to the extent of the interruption of the circulation. Almost always the stroke starts from fine blood vessels and is caused partly by the disease of the vessel walls or the surrounding brain matter, partly by the increased pressure of the blood against the vascular wall.

Your husband, dear Caroline, is probably afflicted by both these factors, judging from the medical history of his mental, his emotional changes, so that we now have this organic psycho syndrome under which he, and you too, are suffering so much.'

Carus had been called by Caroline the same morning that Friedrich was found on the Elbe riverside path leading to Loschwitz, from where he was carried home.

The patient lay motionless, but with open eyes, the right corner of his mouth and his right eyelid sagged, and spittle was dripping on the cushion. His right hand appeared slack and lifeless.

Caroline, helpless and in tears, had summoned the doctor. Then of course the necessary measures were taken.

First the doctor had the patient undressed, elevated his head slightly, wrapped his legs for warmth, then bled him thoroughly to drain the blood from the brain. He also recommended acid enemas, hot foot baths and mustard paste for the calves.

'I believe, dear Caroline,' said Carus to console her, 'our patient will soon be better. For this we must make sure he has regular bowel movements and urination. Also we must insure he has the greatest possible care of the skin to avoid decubitus.'

Caroline wiped her tears with a handkerchief. 'Will he be able to paint again?' she asked. 'Painting is his life, and without it his mind would darken even more and our marriage—I can't think clearly, what would happen to our marriage?'

Carus did not answer immediately. He remembered what Goethe had once said: 'Our life can certainly not be prolonged by the doctors. We live as long as God wills it, but it makes a difference if we live miserably like poor dogs or hale and hearty, and for this a good doctor can do much.'

Hale and hearty—hardly would his friend be that again, since he had not been really well in years. But live as a poor dog, no, he, Carus, would try to do his best as a doctor to prevent it. And he would help him through the long process of decline that he was probably facing. He had not told Caroline what he had known for quite a time: Friedrich was suffering from a life-shortening disease of the brain, which had many causes, organic and psychic. But he could not bring himself to tell her what Friedrich probably had ahead of him, other strokes, paralyses and in the end most likely mental derangement with all its attendant consequences and hardships for the family and Friedrich's wife.

No, he did not believe that the painter would ever recover. All the wondrous life processes which help overcome a disease and lead to convalescence and health can only start from our unconscious, and if our psyche is not capable of the long effort of recovery, we will die.

'Talk to him as often as possible while looking after him, that will strengthen his will to live,' said Carus, when he took leave at the door, and softly stroked her cheek. 'I'll visit again tomorrow morning.'

Caroline did not at once go back into the house but went to her neighbor to pour her heart out. That woman, after listening attentively and also a bit greedily, said that she had a friend in a nearby village who had told her how to care for a patient down with stroke. The afflicted must be positioned so that the healer does not step into his shadow. Then she takes a kind of rough or coarse broom, strokes the patient with it and murmurs:

'Stroke and murder attack,
Then Lord Jesus came and brought you back.
In the name of the Father, the Son and the Holy Spirit.'

If this would not help, there was a second saying:

'The stroke and murder
Went together through a gate so thin,
There came Jesus Christ and helped again.'

Here again the broom must be used diligently, the brushwood of which must be cut by an immaculate virgin during full moon.

Caroline thanked her neighbor, persuaded her not to come visit the patient just yet, and said that Dr. Carus would certainly not tolerate such an interference in his treatment, and she therefore could not follow the neighbor's advice, not even secretly, as the neighbor had said.

After that she went back into the house to look after her husband.

CHAPTER 24

It clanged and resounded when he strode through the half-destroyed passageways. Sometimes he had to stoop down or dodge the bulges and protrusions, and sometimes huge caverns opened up before him which like Gothic cathedrals grew to dusky heights.

Beside him there was roaring and humming like mighty flows in the rhythm of his heartbeat. A bloody red semi-darkness prevailed, which lighted his way.

A small dark man with a black top hat and long coat joined him. It seemed to Friedrich that he walked with a limp. Injured your foot, didn't you, Lucifer, when you fell from heaven. Be quiet, God is gracious, and he does not allow eternal damnation. Your transformation and pardon and those of your followers are part of his plan for the final restoration of the world in its original state and the conversion of all creatures and the end of all punishment and evil and guilt.

Then we will again be part of the holy, inseparable godly nature and of a better world, which the wonderful sun warms with a purer and nobler shine.

Mr. Friedrich, I do not understand. It is my task to help the light and color of the elements take their proper and independent place. Maybe this is the reason you call me Lucifer, the bringer of light.

The only true source of art, Mr. Turner, is our heart, the language of the pure, naïve soul. A thing that does not spring from this source can only be affectation, mannerism. Every true piece of art is conceived in a sacred hour and born in a happy one, which the artist often is not aware of but follows at the inner urge of his heart. Have you, Mr. Turner, this heart?

You are making me impatient, Herr Friedrich. Heart, you are saying and naïve soul. But is art morally bound to heart and subject to conscience?

Hear about my painting The Burning of the Houses of Lords and Commons, 16th October 1843, which I did last year. Really, naïve soul, pure heart and sacred hour! I lived through the nightly catastrophe, no, more than that, I deliberately and full of relish took part watching from a boat on the Thames, for the sake of art and the gruesome-beautiful experience. Westminster Palace was on fire. This grand palace, built by Edward the Confessor and extended by William the Conqueror, already heavily damaged by a fire in 1512 and from then on no longer used as a royal residence. Above the river reflecting the fire and littered by boats the Houses of Parliament are in brightest flames, which rise up to the sky. The glow of the fire is spreading to the right over the bridge. Behind that, whitish-gray clouds of smoke are drifting away. Only to the upper right a small piece of the night-blue sky can be seen. In the foreground there is a milling crowd. On the bridge, too, people have gathered. Can you feel the forceful effect of this scene, even though you have only my spoken description? Can you feel the pleasure, not to say lust, which I felt when painting?

The heat of the fire on the left side is contrasted most sharply with the pale brickwork of the bridge. I gave this scene of destruction a kind of utter unrest. The flaring flames and the black smoke form a restless contrast. The same goes for the boats on the river, how they are gliding away from each other, then gather again, and also the people, who move in different directions. The bridge is no quiet point either, but I have painted it hazy, almost translucent. My image does not lend the details any fixed duration. Yes, listen and be amazed, I, a professor of perspective, abort the rules of perspective and revoke the obligation for spatial relationships in the picture and thereby challenge the basic principles of composition. More than that, the extreme edges of the picture which traditionally do not correspond to each other, if you cover them along the vertical line of the central bridge pillar, you will notice—are connected solely by the wide arc of the embankment line at the bottom of the picture.

The painting is like the world in its devilish chaos and hellish fury raging against the sky, all caused by man.

They walk on, Friedrich keeping some distance to the dark little man because he is afraid of such enormous and uncanny passion in a painter.

Before them the tunnel opens and they reach a flat rocky seashore. Over the sea lies a translucent mist, which would soon be dissolving. Friedrich steps into the small boat, which leaves the stony shore. The Englishman remains on the land and lets the German float away. The boat takes him to the great ship lying at some misty distance. It receives the traveler and carries him swiftly away.

EPILOG

CHAPTER 25

Caspar David Friedrich died in Dresden on May 7, 1840. He had suffered a stroke on June 26, 1835, which almost completely paralyzed him. He took the baths in the warm springs of Teplitz, which was made possible when some of his pictures were purchased by the Russian Imperial Court. These treatments allowed him to work on a small number of new paintings and continue with some already begun. Among them was the enchanting oil Pinewood with Pond. In this picture, as often in his later age he contrasts two sources of light, an earthly and a heavenly one, in order to build a bridge from the present to the eternal.

But the act of painting had become extremely difficult, since he could not place his hand on a support. So a large painting of the Bohemian country remained unfinished in his studio and was preserved by his friend and housemate Dahl.

Carus, who helped sell Friedrich's pictures, wrote to a friend living some distance away in 1839: 'What concerns Friedrich, he lives just so, but paralyzed by a stroke and without working ... Friends have collected some money, which he is very much in need of.'

A portrait done by Caroline Bardua in 1840 shows him at the window looking out toward the Elbe river, bowed, hands slack, beside him the untouched palette. His head is slightly tilted, and his glance seems to be directed to a world beyond.

Vasily Andreyevich Zhukovsky, tutor of crown prince Alexander and intermediary of classical European literature in Russian, wrote about one of his last visits to Friedrich on March 19 in his diary that the latter had wept like a child when he talked about needing help from the Czar, who had promised to aid him should he be in distress. He felt that if he could no longer work, he would soon die and leave his family in poverty.

It might have been a consolation for Friedrich when Zhukovsky selected further drawings to be purchased by the Czar but the support came only after Friedrich's death. It did however benefit his widow and the two younger under-age children, his eldest daughter having already been married at that time.

Johann Christian Dahl wrote in his obituary: 'In no way was Caspar David Friedrich fortune's darling, and he experienced what many deeply gifted people do in their lives, where few understand them rightly and they are misunderstood by most.'

Caspar David Friedrich, the greatest landscape painter of German romanticism, was quickly forgotten. Modern landscape painting, foremost the Düsseldorf school with its realism soon dominated the scene, where Friedrich's melancholic mood and otherworldly symbolism had no place.

It was a Norwegian who would remind the Germans at the beginning of the 1890s.

Andreas Aubert, Dahl's biographer, working through the diaries and letters of Dahl, discovered in them the admiration and even veneration that Dahl had for a German painter in

Dresden named Caspar David Friedrich. So he traveled to Germany to find out what the artistic relationship between the two had been. But he could find no mention of a painter by name of Caspar David Friedrich in Germany.

In 1908, at the Congress on Historical Art in Darmstadt, Aubert told the audience how his search began.

At the National Gallery in Berlin there were no paintings by Friedrich, and he was unknown to the scholars there. So he went to Dresden, where both Friedrich and Dahl had lived. The result was the same, there were no paintings by Friedrich in the Gallery, and in the director's office he again heard, as in Berlin, he must be in error, there was no such painter as described in Germany.

Aubert worked himself into a rage. 'Have you Germans gone completely crazy? In Dahl's letters I can follow Friedrich's life, from these letters I know of his paintings and their contents, and you Germans deny the existence of this artist and tell me I am wrong?' In his excitement he had thumped the table with his fist and shouted his words out, causing the director to shout back. The scene had witnesses, and the shouting was heard by servants in the halls. Then there was a knock on the door, and the old attendant of the anteroom, whose job it was to announce visitors, came in timidly: 'I beg your pardon for interrupting, but I heard the gentlemen talking about Friedrich, Herr Director. We do have Friedrich in the Gallery. When I started here forty years ago, Friedrich hung here, the pictures are in the archives. I can show the gentlemen.' Amazed the men followed the old attendant, who led them to the storage area, and showed them several small paintings. Aubert called: 'But here we have them! I know all these from Dahl's letters. There is Two Men Contemplating the Moon, here are the two Old Heroes' Graves in autumn and in the snow, and there is the Hay Harvesting image.

So Friedrich was rediscovered at the beginning of an artistic epoch of light, color, neo-romanticism and symbolism, and increased longing for naturalness and nature.

Then the thirties and forties of the 20th century witnessed a change in Germany, which brought about an abuse of the personality and work of Friedrich. He was made harbinger and principal witness of a sinister movement which led to his being suspect after the war.

However, since the beginning of the sixties, a fairer assessment has emerged, crowned by the great exhibitions in Hamburg and Dresden in 1974 on the occasion of the 200th anniversary of his birth. Prior to that there had already been an exhibition at the Tate Gallery in London.

Since then Friedrich's international standing has not been in doubt. One of the main reasons may be that people see in his work the existential isolation they are subjected to in the 20th century, an interpretation that would probably not have been shared by the painter.

Caspar David Friedrich was buried on May 10th, 1840 in the Trinitatis cemetery in Dresden.

CHAPTER 26

In 1835 Joseph Mallord William Turner undertook a long journey through Northern Europe and visited, among other cities, Hamburg, Copenhagen, Berlin, Dresden and Prague. From this trip he brought home many sketches made in Dresden and Saxon Switzerland.

Turner, about 7 months younger than Friedrich, survived him by eleven years and died on December 19th, 1851. He was buried in the crypt of St. Paul's Cathedral in London.

Almost from the beginning of his career Turner's art was met with a mixture of praise and rejection, and only the art critic John Ruskin refused to regard Turner exclusively as an interesting eccentric. His letter of defense against Turner's critics grew to become the first volume of his work Modern Painters, published in 1843.

That Turner deviated from his initial precision in representation of the landscape and became increasingly 'indistinct', the paintings seeming to evade any definite interpretation, Ruskin did not see as a shortcoming but the proper expression of the inscrutability of the modern world.

With Turner he was of the opinion that the sublime cannot exist without mysteriousness.

But even Ruskin did not recognize how Turner's art presaged modernist complexity. And when he was commissioned to administer Turner's bequest, he allowed the National Gallery trustees to destroy the 'grossly obscene drawings' which Turner had made during and after his visits to brothels. The drawings, he wrote, could only be 'evidence of the failure of mind'. So, the drawings were burnt.

In 1845 Turner had sent a painting, Walhalla, to a show in Munich. Elizabeth Rigby (later Lady Eastlake) tells of a visit to Queen Anne Street about this time. 'The old gentleman was great fun: his splendid picture of Walhalla had been sent to Munich, there ridiculed as might be expected and returned to him with L7 to pay, and sundry spots upon it: on these Turner laid his odd misshapen thumb in a pathetic way. Mr. Munro (of Novar) suggested they would rub out, and I offered my cambric handkerchief; but the old man edged us away, and stood before his picture like a hen in fury.'

In France Turner was appreciated quite differently. Claude Monet and Camille Pissaro visited London in 1871 and discovered Turner for themselves, who in this way exercised an important influence on the development of impressionism with all its far-reaching consequences for modern art.

Turner's legacy as a painter was immense. He left in fact 370 unsold oil paintings. In all there were 95,800 water colors, drawings, oil paintings, engravings and plates.

Since he thought that all his works had to be contemplated as a group, as one entity, to be properly understood, he tried to keep his pictures together, even repurchasing them himself sometimes for prices higher than those at which he had sold them. Towards the end of his life he rejected an offer of L100,000 for the pictures in his gallery.

He wanted his works to belong to the whole nation, exhibited in a gallery open to everybody. This wish was only fulfilled in the last quarter of the 20th century, when the Tate Gallery, which was opened in 1879, was extended by the Clore Gallery, which now contains the most comprehensive collection of Turner's works.

There is no proof that Caspar David Friedrich and Joseph Mallord William Turner met in Dresden, nor that they had ever heard of each other.

About the Author

Christoph Werner was born in the East German city of Halle on the Saale river and raised as the son of a Lutheran minister. He studied English and German at Martin Luther University at Halle and worked at various universities in East and West Germany before retiring to live in Weimar.

He has written four novels and numerous short stories and essays.

ALSO BY CHRISTOPH WERNER

SHADOWS OF MY FATHER
THE MEMOIRS OF MARTIN LUTHER'S SON
A Novel
Translated by Michael Leonard

An enthralling and original novel that brings to life one of Christianity's most significant figures, Martin Luther, and the tumultuous world of late medieval Germany that shaped him—and was reshaped by him—told by his youngest son, Paul.

Unwilling to join his father's fanatical disciples, Paul became critical of his famous father's critiques and instead turned his interest and intellect to science and medicine. Yet Martin Luther remained a presence that haunted Paul's life and transformed his world.

Shadows of My Father paints a vivid and atmospheric picture of Martin Luther, including his day-to-day life, his break with the Catholic Church, and his singular dedication in sustaining the Reformation. It is also a portrait of a son raised in a harsh religious household who turns his faith to saving lives instead of souls, eventually becoming a royal doctor.

Christoph Werner vividly re-creates the world of sixteenth-century Germany, a time of wars and famines when a Kaiser battles to keep an empire together and when faith and tradition clash with education and reason—giving birth to superstition and shaking the foundations of a Catholic Church already riven by internal conflict. A thoughtful, insightful lens into one of the most famous figures, one of the most profound historical events, and one of the most turbulent periods in our past, *Shadows of My Father* reveals an intriguing, historically accurate, and all-too-human side of Martin Luther and his lasting legacy.

Harper Legend 2017
ISBN: 978-0062846525 (Paperback)
Ebook available

BOOKS BY CHRISTOPH WERNER

Der Bronstein-Defekt und andere Geschichten

Schloss am Strom. Die Geschichte vom Leben und Sterben des Baumeisters Karl Friedrich Schinkel

Um ewig einst zu leben. Caspar David Friedrich und Joseph Mallord William Turner. Roman

To Live in all Eternity. Caspar David Friedrich and Joseph Mallord William Turner. A Novel.

Buckingham Palace. Roman

Wintermorgen — Geschichten und Geschichtliches

Paulus Luther. Sein Leben von ihm selbst aufgeschrieben. Wahrhaftiger Roman

Shadows of My Father. The Memoirs of Martin Luther's Son. A Novel

Zeitfracht Medien GmbH
Ferdinand-Jühlke-Straße 7
99095 Erfurt, Deutschland
produktsicherheit@kolibri360.de